THE

COMPASS

Jeanine —
Wishing you happiness
always wherever your
compass directs you.
Happy reading!

THE
COMPASS

DEBORAH RADWAN

Deborah Radwan

iUniverse, Inc.
Bloomington

The Compass

iUniverse books may be ordered through booksellers or by contacting:

iUniverse
1663 Liberty Drive
Bloomington, IN 47403
www.iuniverse.com
1-800-Authors (1-800-288-4677)

ISBN: 978-1-4697-0623-8 (sc)
ISBN: 978-1-4697-0624-5 (hc)
ISBN: 978-1-4697-0625-2 (ebk)

Library of Congress Control Number: 2012900066

Printed in the United States of America

iUniverse rev. date: 01/16/2012

In memory of my parents,
Chet and Arline

"In the beginning God created the heavens and the earth;
the earth was waste and void:
darkness covered the abyss,
and the spirit of God was stirring above the waters." Genesis 1:1-2

"Then God said, 'Let the earth bring forth vegetation:
seed bearing plants and all kinds of fruit trees that bear fruit
containing their seed.'
And so it was . . . God saw that it was good." Genesis 1:11-12

"When the Lord God made the earth and the heavens,
there was not yet any field shrub on the earth
nor had the plants of the field sprung up,
for the Lord God had sent no rain on the earth and
there was no man to till the soil; but a mist rose from the earth and
watered all the surface of the ground." Genesis 2:4-6

"The Lord God planted a garden in Eden, to the east,
and he put there the man he had formed.
The Lord God made to grow out of the ground all kinds of trees
pleasant to the sight and good for food, the tree of life also in the midst
of the garden, and
the tree of the knowledge of good and evil." Genesis 2:8-9

"Now when they were in the field, Cain turned against his brother
Abel and slew him. Then the Lord said to Cain, 'Where is your
brother Abel?' He answered, 'I do not know. Am I my brother's
keeper?' And the Lord said, 'What have you done? The voice of your
brother's blood cries to me from the ground.'" Genesis 4:8-10

Summer 1995, a neighborhood in East Los Angeles

Chapter 1

A grizzled-looking old man, Jacob leaned back on his knees, rubbed the soil from his hands onto stained pants, and hoisted himself from the ground with considerable effort. He steadied his upward progression with the aid of a hoe that looked as worn as he did. His forward-bent shadow leaned to one side like a tree that grows toward the sun. Clinging white-knuckled to his staff, he allowed it to bear the brunt of his weight until he could properly straighten his spine—a task that was harder with each passing day. Jacob reached into his back pocket and pulled out a rag to wipe the sweat and dirt that had settled into the wrinkles and creased brow of his weathered face. Ironically, the thin, white castoff, discolored and soiled, displayed a monogrammed "L" in the corner, betraying better, more distinguished days.

Hearing a ruckus coming from down the street, Jacob turned toward it. *The usual routine*, he thought, shaking his head in disapproval. School had just let out for the summer. Jacob watched as a swarm of boys on bicycles rode by, some using language that no decent boys of that age should know, much less be using in casual conversation. The anger and the power in the boys' voices scared him, but he looked at them with a steady eye, hiding his fear.

"What are you staring at, Jew man?" one boy yelled at him as they rode by. A second one spit in his direction, saying, "Filthy kike." Another boy thrust out his arm and lifted his middle finger. The rest of the boys laughed—except for one. That boy stared back at Jacob with an equally unflinching eye.

Jacob straightened and stood tall next to his hoe, his head slightly lifted, his chin defiant—but said nothing. A shiver ran down his spine. His eyes were locked on the boy holding up the rear of the group, the boy with the fixed eyes and still expression scrutinizing him intently as he rode by. The boy then turned his attention back to the group and peddled faster to catch up to the others who were several bike lengths ahead.

It wasn't until the boys were out of sight that Jacob relaxed again, his body resisting the impulse to tremble.

Lumbering down the drive, he complained to himself that he was an old man in an old neighborhood. *Why hadn't he left?* he asked himself again for the hundredth time now, as he looked up and down the street, disappointed at what he saw. The pleasant neighborhood he bought into in the early fifties was now run-down and dilapidated, and a bad element had infiltrated the old comfortable homes. Mrs. Jefferson was a widow who couldn't afford her electric bill much less home improvements on her husband's pension; Mr. and Mrs. Sanchez were too busy taking care of their grandchildren and great grandchildren to worry about the blistering paint that marred their house; and Jacob didn't even want to think about what was going on in the house next to them. That house was once pristine with a manicured lawn and flowers along the sidewalk and a sign on the porch that read "The Myers." Jacob remembered them as a lovely family that took great pride in their little "Shangri-La," as they dubbed it. They believed they had a piece of the American dream. Now, there was a car parked on the lawn, a ripped sofa on the porch, and a flag being used as a curtain. Rough and raw-looking people came and went at odd hours, day and night—in, then out ten minutes later. Tattooed with closely shaved heads, they would often screech away. "Hooligans," Jacob muttered to himself.

4

But even as Jacob asked himself why he stayed, he knew it was because of his longtime neighbors, Frederick and Yoshito, and the garden the three of them created from the thirsty and barren soil once overrun with dead and brittle weeds.

For decades, the expansive and hidden yards behind their individual homes that sat side by side had been left untended; they were too big to handle and therefore ignored, abandoned, and left to die.

One March morning, a dozen years back now, maybe more, Frederick heard his dead Negro ancestors singing for the first time. He said their deep soulful voices rose out of the yard singing "We Are Climbing Jacob's Ladder." Although he couldn't see them, he sensed they were working in the garden the way they had worked the fields in the Deep South, where his people came from. Their voices were filled with joy and praise. From that day forward, Frederick worked in his yard from early in the morning, when just a hint of brightness lit up the eastern sky, until long after the sun's luster had dimmed. In those early days, Jacob and Yoshito wondered if he ever stopped to sleep.

Frederick didn't always hear the singing now, but he made up for it with his own raised voice. In the beginning, when there was much to be done, Frederick heard them all the time, blending their voices with his, pushing him forward to dig out pathways, plant flowers and trees of every variety, and grow herbs and vegetables. Now, the singing came when he least expected it, when he was just about to give up hope of ever hearing them again. In those moments, Frederick's voice was louder and richer as he sang in harmony with a choir only he could hear. But since that first day, he claimed to feel part of them, linked to his past as he worked by their unseen sides. Over time, Frederick's large, dead, and parched rectangular yard began to mold into paths and patches and change in color, texture, and richness. The hard became soft; the brown turned green; the dull became bright; and the dry was rich and nourished. He claimed a similar metamorphosis had taken hold of his soul. In the intervening years, Frederick seemed happier, younger, and stronger—for an old man.

That same magical summer that Frederick heard the singing, Yoshito claimed to hear his dying trees and withering bushes whispering to him in a parched voice that they were thirsty, and dutifully, he gave them drink. Feeling honored that his plants should talk to him and that he had been given the gift to hear them, he followed Frederick's lead. Before long, Yoshito began transforming his yard. Soon after, they tore down the fence between their homes and began working together on one beautiful Eden.

They're getting old and they're going crazy, hearing voices, Jacob often thought. "Old men's ramblings," he would grumble to himself, shaking his head in disbelief at their nonsense.

As for himself, transforming his garden had just given him something to do, something to pass the time. Perhaps he had needed something beautiful in his life, and the garden seemed to fill a void. So he joined Frederick and Yoshito in creating his little piece of paradise. Jacob heard no sweet ancestors singing and no whispered voices from the garden. He only heard the daily chorus of the birds in his trees and he was satisfied with that.

Jacob did, however, hear voices in his dreams. They were unwelcome visitors on whom the door would not close. Even after all these decades, he sometimes heard cruel, rough German voices from the past shouting orders, calling him names, ordering him and his father to go to the right, his mother and sister to the left. He'd looked back into a sea of crying women and children as he and his father were pushed with other men and older boys out of sight—and that was the last he saw of his mother and sister. His dreams varied slightly, but it was always cold, rainy, and gray, and he was always in that same place. He always felt the same terror and nearly always awakened crying feeling like a boy again. Even in his dreams, those long dead voices sounded real, frightening him still, inviting the memories that he pushed down during the day to seep back to his consciousness as he slept vulnerable to their power.

During the day, Jacob found respite in his garden and in the companionship of his dear neighbors. Not many had seen the Eden that lay hidden behind their homes, but those who had could not dispute the results whatever the motivation, even if it was senility.

And, despite whatever madness invaded Frederick's and Yoshito's senses, they were his friends. Through some great miracle the three of them had been placed next door to each other on this earth, only to find after years of gaining trust that they shared similar histories; dark histories they did not share with many. They understood each other. And so their relationships evolved over the years from neighbors to friends and then to family, as if they were brothers sharing one history instead of three similar histories. Jacob knew how lucky he was to have them in his life. They were good men—even if they were going mad. "The geriatric musketeers," Jacob would say whenever the three of them had worked together on some project, like when they first built their raised beds for their vegetable garden behind Frederick's house.

In their garden, the seasons passed easily, each changing the complexion and colors of the garden. The work never seemed to end. The more they planted and weeded and hoed, the more they found to plant, weed, and hoe. But their labors filled their days, and they were rewarded with the opening of a rose, the bloom of a daffodil, the drape of purple wisteria, the smell of fresh cilantro and lavender, and the sweetness and juiciness of a homegrown tomato. Simply, they had come to love their garden, their Eden, as they called it. They recalled that God had created the Garden of Eden from nothing, much as they had done with the dead earth that once was their backyards. At the end of a fine day, like today, after the watering and cleaning up was done, the singing faded, the plants satiated, and the birds retired, they would sit in their garden and enjoy its coolness and beauty and wonder, until the darkness enfolded them reminding them of their pillows and the feathery dreams that awaited them.

While the others welcomed sleep, Jacob resisted it, knowing his nightmares would come if not tonight then tomorrow. However reconciled to them he had become, he could only hope that they would strike as close to dawn as possible so as not to ruin an entire night of sleep.

Jacob's garden was as beautiful as the other's, but he had not yet torn down the fence between his garden and the rest of Eden.

He needed help; he couldn't do it alone. An old man like himself, or even two old men, could not wrestle that wire fence down; it seemed to have the strength of Hercules. Frederick said he would get help from someone at his church. Jacob had to remember to ask him about it—but then again, he was in no hurry.

Squinting, and then cupping his hand over his eyes, Jacob looked up at the bright sky rather than at his watch and decided from the angle of the sun that it was close to three o'clock in the afternoon. He confirmed his suspicion by measuring the size of the all too familiar and still-bent shadow that sprouted from his feet and stretched across the blistering hot driveway, noting that his image slightly wavered like a mirage in the sweltering heat. The air screamed its stillness and summer oppression, and it was only the end of June. In that still air, he noted the absence of the whistling and chattering birds that normally filled his ears when the day was young and realized they had been silent several hours—further evidence that the day was well situated somewhere around the mid-afternoon hour.

Even after all these years, Jacob still wondered where his feathery friends went when the sun was too high and the afternoons too long. They would not reappear until the sun fell lower in the sky, the brightness became muted, and the air cooled. Then they would keep him company again for a few hours more until sunset bid them home. He sometimes wondered if they retired to a place over the rainbow like the song said. His good-humored friends joked with him about this theory, but since none of them had seen a bird sleep, he knew a place like that must exist.

As the sun scorched his back through his sweat-soaked cotton undershirt, Jacob thought, *It's too hot for them; they're off sleeping. I should take a lesson from them.* But instead of feeling branded and burned from the sun, the heat seemed more to him like the luxury of a hot bath surrounding him and settling in around his bones and joints, easing the exertions of the day. Each morning, his movements were slow and heavy, his muscles stiff. Then, as the sun gathered strength and intensity, warming the dirt in which he crawled from sunup to sundown, he found his body loosening and ridding itself of the chill that accompanied his dreams as he slept. His old body relished the comfort that heat brought to his movements, the years it took away, and the cold memories it suppressed. It was not the raised mercury that made him feel branded, but the black number tattooed on the inside of his forearm that neither soap nor time could take away and that a summer tan could not hide. *I should have had that removed a long time ago,* he thought again as he had so many times over the decades, but he never did.

Jacob drew his attention back to the patch of planters along the driveway where he had been working all day to critique his own handiwork. *Ah,* he corrected himself, *God's handiwork.* He had merely arranged God's colorful and leafy creations, rejuvenated the soil with some mulch, and seized the evil weeds from their strangling tendencies. He gave a nod of approval to no one but himself.

Next door, Frederick had gone indoors to prepare iced tea for all of them. "The nectar of the gods," Frederick called it. Jacob would routinely shake his head and say, "It's only a tea bag and some water, my dramatic friend."

Yoshito had gone to the nursery hours earlier for more bags of peat moss and manure for the project he was going to start the next day. *Must have gotten caught up talking to the hydrangeas at the nursery,* Jacob mused to himself. He took some small delight in teasing his old friends, and they let him enjoy himself at their expense.

Jacob looked at the next planter over and thought that he must amend that soil and pull any weeds tomorrow. From behind him, he heard Frederick's voice at the fence, and it startled him.

"Here's your tea, Jacob," Frederick said, as he reached over the chain link fence that separated his part of Eden from the whole. Jacob took a cool, long draught from the glass. Satisfied, he and Frederick sought shade nearby, each on their own side of the fence.

"You did a fine job on that planter. Just a little water and those new flowers will take off in no time. What is that yellow one, yarrow?" Frederick asked.

Jacob just nodded, still inspecting his work.

Frederick continued. "Oh, I've got a teenage boy coming to help take down this fence. His mother is anxious to fill his summer with something other than the crowd he's started to hang with, so I offered him a little cash for some honest hard work. His mother is grateful."

"You may be asking for trouble, my friend. Teenager? Bad crowd? I don't like the sound of it."

Jacob found himself thinking back to the boys on the bikes; how the taunting and the hostile eyes of those neighborhood boys that gawked at him had reminded him of the young men in Germany so long ago, after it was no longer safe to be Jewish. It didn't matter that he was ten thousand miles and fifty-five years removed from it. Jew, "Jude," the way they spit out the word, was the same. Jacob wondered how such young boys then and now could have so much anger and hatred inside them. *Too young, too young*, Jacob thought shaking his head.

Jacob knew that this was not Germany in the 1930s and 1940s. It was not that he was old, or a Jew. He could have been anything—Mexican, Puerto Rican, Asian, Black, white, short, tall, fat, skinny, blond, what did they call it . . . gay?—it didn't matter. It was that he was not whatever they thought they were. But this wasn't much consolation. He'd seen too much, knew what could happen, to shrug it off easily. *But what could he do?* Jacob wondered, feeling as helpless now as he had then. Now he was going to have some troubled teenager working in his Eden? He didn't like the idea.

"It'll be fine, Jacob. His mother is a good woman. The boy's father left them when he was just three. He just hasn't had much direction, that's all. Needs to see what some hard work can get you—a little spending money, the feeling of accomplishment, being part of something. You know."

Jacob waved him off. "I think we'll never get this fence down. But what do I know? Let us try Mr. Teenage Big Shot. When does he start?"

"This Saturday, bright and early. I'll be here to help; Yoshito, too, if we need him."

"All right, Frederick. I don't like the idea, but we'll see if we can give Mr. Know-It-All Teenager something to do, see if he sticks with it." Jacob handed back his now empty glass to his friend and headed for the hose to wash away the dirt that clung to his hands and spewed out onto the drive from the planter.

Chapter 2

Saturday morning came early and Rudy arrived late and begrudgingly. He didn't want to be there and had told his mother so, but when they'd fought, she'd cried. That was still one thing he couldn't do, was make his mama cry. He was already thirteen, and the time was coming when he would become a man; and he couldn't be taking no orders from his mama. What would his friends say if they knew he was doing work for the old Jew man? He'd had to make up a story of how he was spending his time; otherwise he'd have a hard time hanging with the group, being one of them. More than anything else, he wanted to belong to something. He was tired of being a nothing; tired of living in a small box that was too hot in the summer and too cold in the winter, of being in the world of the have-nots—tired of having bars on the windows at home, of feeling like he was a victim. The group he was with now taught him what it was like to have power over things and people. They told him to take what he wanted, because no one was going to hand it to him—he deserved it. That seemed a whole lot smarter than praying for things in church on Sunday. His mama seemed to think that the answers to her prayers would fall into her hands like manna from heaven. His mother let millions of rosary beads slide through her fingers, each with a prayer up to heaven, and for what? To have nothing, to be nothing? There'd been no answers to any prayers as far as he could tell. All those hours his mother had spent on her knees amounted to nothing. Even now, he was going to have to work like a dog in the heat of the day over how many weeks, and for what, a few measly bucks?

Just the other day, he shoplifted a pocketknife. It wasn't the one he wanted, but it was his first time and good practice. The guys told him that he seemed to have a talent—real slick—and that he was better than that stupid store owner who had trouble speaking English. Well, he had lost this battle with his mama, but he would win the war. *So help me God*, he thought.

Rudy was just getting ready to knock at the Jew man's door when a tall, slim, black man waved out to him, calling out his name from next door like they were old friends.

"Hey, Rudy! Wait up." The boy looked at the old black man approaching with dislike knowing he was the one who had gotten him this stupid job. It was all his fault that he was there instead of having fun with his friends. *Well, he may have picked cotton in the fields*, Rudy thought, *but no one is going to push me down. No one.* Rudy said nothing.

Extending his hand, Frederick said, "Hi, Rudy. I'm Frederick. I know your mother. I want to thank you for helping Jacob with his fence. I'm afraid we're just too old to tackle a big job like this. A big strong boy like you shouldn't have much trouble though. You'll have it out in no time."

Rudy reluctantly shook Frederick's hand, but he didn't like it, especially when Frederick slapped him lightly on the shoulder, like they were old friends who had just shared the punch line to a joke that amused them both. He didn't say anything in return, just stared through narrow, black shark eyes. Frederick appeared to ignore, accept, or be oblivious to Rudy's coldness. Rudy couldn't figure out which.

"Let's see if we can get Jacob out here," Frederick said as he banged on the front screen door.

Slowly, the heavy wood door on the other side of the security screen opened. The house was dark inside, and Rudy couldn't make out anything except the dark bulky figures of heavy furniture until the shape of a stocky man blocked his view. *The Jew man,* Rudy thought.

"Ah, here is our helper. I am Jacob. And what is your name?" a voice inquired as the heavy metal screen door swung open and Jacob stepped out onto the porch.

Frederick answered for him. "Jacob, this is Rudy. He's here to give us a hand." Rudy said nothing as Jacob looked him up and down, knowing he recognized him as the boy on the bike, the boy with the stare.

"Well, let's see if you are willing to work hard." The three of them walked off the porch and turned around the corner of the house up the driveway to the back yard. For a moment, the expression on Rudy's face softened; his eyes widened as he was unable to hide his surprise. He had no idea what beauty lay behind that small, rundown house. In fact, he had never seen anything so beautiful in his short life; he didn't know that beauty like this could coexist with the shabbiness of this neighborhood that he had begun to hate. Not only was Jacob's garden lush and green and full of colors, but he could see through the chain link fence that it was the same in Frederick's yard next door, as well as the one owned by the old Jap. Rudy noticed there was no fence separating their properties and wondered why. He was suddenly aware of birds singing and that the temperature seemed nearly ten degrees cooler than the front yard where he had just been. Rudy was moved in a way he had never known but tried to hide his astonishment and approval.

Frederick's strong arm around his shoulder steered him toward the fence that needed to be pulled out. Now he understood that Jacob's yard would no longer be separate from the other two yards, but he still didn't understand why.

"Cat got your tongue?" Jacob inquired. Rudy shook his head and looked down. Impatiently, Jacob continued. "Look me in the eye when we talk, young man, and we'll get along much better. I know you can do that." Rudy looked up and held his gaze, more in defiance than in a conciliatory gesture, understanding that Jacob was making a reference to the other day. Jacob went on. "You can never trust a man who won't look you in the eye. Remember that." Rudy nodded, making a point to look at Jacob.

"Jacob, give the boy a chance. Maybe he takes a bit of time to warm to strangers." Excusing himself, Frederick smiled and said he would be back later to check up on the progress.

Jacob led Rudy over to the fence. "This is where your work begins. I will help you as much as I can, but I am an old man. You will need to dig a trench on either side in order to pull out the fence. Frederick, Yoshito, and I will help you when you get to that point. And try not to step on any plants or flowers while you're working. Any questions?"

Rudy just shook his head.

"Okay, Mr. Talkative. Let's get started."

Rudy followed Jacob to a shed where Jacob kept some shovels, thinking with resignation that the sooner he started, the sooner this would be over and he could get the hell out of there. *What a way to spend his summer*, he thought.

Rudy kept his eyes down through the morning, saying nothing, and with every dig into the dirt, he begrudged what his friends were doing. He also found out quickly that this was harder work than he had expected. Very soon, sweat was pouring off of him. It didn't help that every time he wiped the sweat from his eyes, dirt got in them. Before long, his shirt tail was filthy and wet from wiping his face. Around eleven o'clock, Jacob told him that if he used a different shovel and wore gloves, the work might go faster. Rudy stopped, clearly frustrated and angry. *Back off, old man,* he thought, but he said, "I thought you hired me to do the job? Do you want me to do this or not? What makes you think your way is better than mine, huh?" Jacob appeared to cringe and said nothing. Rudy felt good about that. "Stupid, old man," Rudy muttered under his breath, unsure if Jacob heard as he went back to work with more determination.

The morning crawled by, as did the early afternoon. It was now moving toward the hottest part of the day. Jacob offered him a pastrami sandwich around one o'clock. Rudy didn't want to take anything from Jacob; it might look like a sign of weakness. However, he was famished. Still, he could not bring himself to say yes, particularly after their confrontation that morning. Jacob sat down on some nearby rickety wooden chairs under the broad limbs of a nearby tree. Rudy couldn't remember ever eating pastrami before, and as he watched Jacob take a bite, he wondered what it might taste like. It looked really good, or maybe he was just really hungry. Jacob watched him from cautious eyes.

"Here, at least have some iced tea." Smiling to himself, Jacob said, "Frederick calls this the nectar of the gods. I will admit that it does taste good and can kill a thirst, but you must not tell him I said so."

Rudy watched Jacob fill the glass, his mouth feeling gritty and dry from working in the dirt. He was already salivating as the amber liquid poured into the glass. Rudy did not meet Jacob's eyes when he held out the already sweating glass, but instead, he fixated on a tattoo on the inside of his forearm. It was a number. Jacob saw him looking at it. Rudy wondered if Jacob could read the question in his eyes: *What does that number mean?* Jacob's expression seemed to soften toward him, but he said nothing.

Rudy finished out the day around four o'clock. He had made some progress digging the trench a few feet, but he had a long way to go. The yards were at least one hundred and fifty feet long. Who would have thought there was so much room behind these small houses? This was not going to be a short summer job—this would take all of his vacation time.

"We will see you Monday," said Jacob to Rudy's back as he walked down the drive.

A minute or two later, Frederick walked up the driveway saying, "I saw Rudy leave. How'd it go?"

Jacob told him, "We won't see him again," then turned around to put the shovels away.

Rudy did not come back on Monday or the three days after that. That Monday night, Frederick and Yoshito were sitting in their Eden with Jacob, watching the sky darken and the stars appear.

"Just as well," said Jacob. "Nothing but trouble anyway." The others didn't say anything in response.

Jacob had felt very old these past few days. He was mad that he did not stand up to Rudy when he smarted off, but Rudy had reminded him of the unspoken madness of the past that had chased him for decades. It jumped out in front of him like a ghost scaring him with its clarity. He wanted to wipe it away like the soil from his brow but couldn't—especially when Rudy rang his doorbell that Friday.

Jacob controlled his surprise. "Well, Mr. Talkative; decided to come back, did you?" Rudy shrugged as Jacob walked out the front door to escort him to the back. "Okay, you know where the shovels are. But let's get something clear. This is not a come-if-you-feel-like-it job. No doubt you don't want to be here; I think that's pretty clear. But you are either here or you aren't. You choose. We can tell that you do not like spending your time with us old men. Well, that's the job. But I do expect respect and no talking back or complaining. If you can't do that, then you may as well go home. Understood?" Rudy nodded in defeat, relinquishing the last of the rope in this tug of war. Jacob and his mama had won. Jacob turned away, shaken but victorious at having taken a stand against this lone angry boy. He had done it; he had done it.

Chapter 3

Rudy didn't like being at Jacob's house, but he was determined not to be a quitter. Besides, he could use the money. God knows his mother didn't have any to spare. He would just stick it out, do the work, and get out of there. At least, that is what he was telling himself.

Truth is that something had happened in the last couple of days that had scared him. He had been with his friends hanging out in the park just as darkness was settling. Some kids from school were playing basketball nearby. They were the smart kids, the good kids. As darkness fell, the game broke up and they started heading for home. One of the kids who was always studying and getting good grades was walking alone. Rudy and his friends started to follow him, tease him, and give him a bad time. At first it was funny, but before long, Rudy's friends were shoving the boy. Next thing Rudy knew, they were hitting him—hard. The boy was lying on the ground crying, defenseless, blood dripping from his nose. It was the oldest of Rudy's friends doing most of the punching, and the rest of the guys were cheering him on, wishing they could get in a good punch. Rudy saw a crazed look in his friend's eyes as he told the boy on the ground that if he told anyone, next time he wouldn't survive what they had in store for him. Rudy was stunned. All he could do was watch in the background and then run away with the rest of them, afraid of being caught. Truth be told, the hatred in his friend's eyes and the look on his face scared Rudy. It was one thing to steal a pocket knife from a store; it was something else to physically hurt and scare someone who was just minding his own business. It made Rudy stop and wonder what he was getting into. He wanted to be someone, but this, this seemed wrong. Inside, he was ashamed he had just stood by and done nothing. Rudy should have said something or tried to pull his friend off that kid, but he didn't. He was too afraid.

Not knowing what to do, Rudy decided to go back to Jacob's. It would give him time to think and provide an excuse for not being around his friends. Besides, he hadn't told his mama that he'd ditched the job. Maybe now she would never have to know.

Rudy rarely spoke at Jacob's house—just a question here or there, a comment on the heat, and to ask for a glass of water. Jacob seemed to respect his silence, and that was just fine with him. From all that he could see, these three old men really liked each other and got along. It was kind of funny to be around them, different than what he was used to. Every now and again, they would talk about something from the past that piqued his interest, but he would never ask a question. Didn't want to give the impression that he cared. He didn't. "Was just curious—that's all.

The tattoo on Jacob's arm had a story, and he wanted to hear it, but Jacob never mentioned it. Finally, one day while they were all eating lunch, he found himself staring at it again as Jacob reached for a pitcher of tea that Frederick had made. Jacob caught him again in his stare and finally said, "Do you know what this is?" Jacob was pointing to the number emblazoned on the inside of his forearm. Rudy, embarrassed, shook his head no. "Sometime, maybe, I will tell you a very terrible story, but not today." Rudy was disappointed but just shrugged like it was no big deal. Inside, his hunger grew to hear the story. Frederick picked up on it but said nothing. Yoshito just watched the boy, wondering if he could be saved from the life he was tumbling toward.

Now Rudy had a reason to show up each day. Each day that he strolled up the driveway, he thought that maybe today he would hear Jacob's story. Sometime before the fence was down, he would get the old man to tell it to him.

Chapter 4

Rudy showed up on a Wednesday a couple weeks into the job only to find that Jacob was not feeling well.

As he had resigned himself to working for the summer, Rudy's anger at being there lessened. When he asked Frederick if Jacob was okay, Rudy surprised himself at his own genuine concern.

"He just had a rough night. Didn't get much sleep. Just needs some rest. I'll be helping you today," Frederick said, greeting him as he walked up the driveway.

"Let's go over to my side of the fence so as not to disturb Jacob." Rudy followed dutifully around the front of Jacob's house and up the driveway to the back of Frederick's house. It was odd to see it from the other side of the fence. It was the same, but different too. It was the difference of looking at a picture and being in the picture.

Still, Rudy was disappointed about this turn of events. And though Frederick was nice enough, he knew it was going to be a long day, and now it would not be *the* day he would learn Jacob's story. For some reason, he couldn't get that tattoo out of his head. Maybe Frederick knew the story.

Rudy began digging the trench along Frederick's side of the fence. As he worked, Frederick sang one spiritual after the next while weeding nearby. Rudy was ready to go crazy. *All right already,* he thought. As soon as there was a break between songs, Rudy stole the opportunity to ask, "Hey, do you know the story about that tattoo on Jacob's arm?" Frederick stopped and considered his response before looking up.

"Yes, yes, I do, but I think it is Jacob's story to share when he is ready, don't you?"

Rudy shrugged and went back to digging the trench, wondering what the big deal was. He noticed that Frederick still seemed to have something on his mind.

"There are many terrible things in this world, Rudy; people who allow evil and darkness to invade their souls and who do and say terrible things to other people who look different, talk differently, belong to different religions . . . I know you are aware of that. It's a very frightening thing when this hatred takes hold, and it becomes organized. It's like some kind of crazy boulder falling down the side of the hill that picks up things in its way and becomes bigger and bigger, or like a contagious plague that ravishes the weak-minded. It's hard to stop that kind of thing. It can be done, but it takes a long time. I know what I am talking about, believe me."

Rudy looked back at Frederick but was thinking of his friends in the park. It was almost as if Frederick had been watching what had happened to that scared boy left crying on the ground—as if he knew his secret. But whatever Frederick was talking about had happened to him.

"You want to hear a story? I've got one for you. Come and sit down here and rest a spell while I tell you about my family."

Intrigued, Rudy moved away from the fence, wiped is forehead on his sleeve and sat down at a small table. With iced tea in hand, thus began the education of Rudy, Mr. Talkative.

Chapter 5

"Have you heard of the Civil Rights movement, Rudy?" He nodded, yes; he knew something about it. "Well, this story begins long before there were civil rights. They used to call us colored people. When I was growing up, colored people, well, we didn't have any rights. Do you know we couldn't drink out of the same drinking faucets or use the same bathrooms as the white people? If we did, we could go to jail or get beat up, or even worse."

Frederick paused and looked away, staring as if trying to see something that he couldn't quite focus on. Rudy had, of course, heard these stories but didn't know if he quite believed them. Yet, here was someone who had lived it. He waited for Frederick to go on.

"Thing was there was not much we could do about it if we wanted to stay safe. It's just the way it was for a long time. I grew up in the South. My people, my great-grandparents, were slaves and picked cotton on a plantation most of their lives. They were around for the Emancipation Proclamation. Did you learn about the Emancipation Proclamation in school?"

Not waiting for a response, Frederick cocked his head, listening to something he heard stirring in the garden. "Come with me, Rudy." Rudy put down his sweaty glass and followed Frederick toward the center of his garden, wondering what was going on. Frederick continued talking, not waiting for them to reach their destination.

"I never knew my great-grandparents but heard stories about them from my grandparents. Sometimes I hear them and my other ancestors singing in the garden. Did Jacob tell you that? He likes to have a little fun teasing me about it; thinks I'm crazy." Frederick laughed shaking his head.

"I know it sounds funny to you, Rudy, but this land was nothing but dirt and weeds more than a decade ago. It was hearing them one morning out my back door that made me want to come out and work the soil as they had a century before."

Rudy wondered if he was kidding but was just trying to keep up with Frederick's fast pace. The old guy could move pretty fast; must be those long legs.

"You've probably been wondering why I sing so much? When I sing with them . . . well, it's a magical feeling. When I sing alone, I still feel like they are near me, and I wonder if today will be the day I hear them again."

Frederick stopped short and pointed to an area ahead of them. "Actually, I hear them now; it's coming from over there. Listen, Rudy; close your eyes and just listen."

Rudy looked incredulously at Frederick, but then changed his expression when he could see that Frederick was serious. Feeling ridiculous, Rudy closed his eyes, uncomfortable and almost snickering yet yearning to hear something. All he could hear was leaves rustling.

"I don't hear nothin'," Rudy responded finally.

"That's okay. You will one day," Frederick replied confidently and started walking again towards the place that was the heart of Eden.

Stopping, Frederick pointed to a three-foot pedestal surrounded by rose bushes with pink-colored blooms. On top of the dais was a compass covered by a glass dome. "Right here, right in this spot is where I dug out the first weeds. Right here is where I felt I was working alongside them. As the heat rose up, I almost felt it was their hot breath. Here was where their voices were the loudest. That experience has turned out to be a great thing in more ways than one—changed my life."

Frederick hesitated, reflecting on what he had just said. Rudy pointed to the pedestal and compass and asked, "What's this?" What he really meant to ask was why Frederick had a compass in the yard.

Frederick seemed to understand and replied, "I wanted to mark the spot where this all began." He spread his arms wide to encompass all of Eden. "Yoshito gave me the idea. Did you know that in medieval times they thought a compass was akin to the eye of God? That Yoshito is a font of information. I like the idea that God is watching over this place, but I also think there is something safe and grounding about a compass. It helps you find your way home. That's what my ancestors did for me with this garden—they grounded me to this place."

Frederick took in a deep breath and looked around at the beautiful garden surrounding them; he couldn't imagine it being any other way. "Takes your breath away, doesn't it?" Frederick asked, and Rudy nodded. He had to agree that it was unbelievable.

"C'mon, let's rest under this tree, sit on that fine old bench." Frederick motioned toward the weathered bench that rested itself under the canopy of the Sycamore that was at the far back of the lot. Rudy followed, and as they brushed against the lavender, its smell was released and filled the air. It was intoxicating.

"Now, let me start again, but at the beginning. Growing up in the South in the first half of the century was not easy for a black man. I was the only son of Calvin and Lilly Washington. They named me after the great Frederick Douglas. You know Frederick Douglas?" Rudy thought the name was familiar but wasn't sure if he did or didn't. He was never that good at paying attention in school.

"My momma was the prettiest woman I have ever seen. When I was a little boy, I was so proud of her. No one had a mother that was prettier than mine. My daddy adored her. Used to call her 'Sugar' when he was wanting to romance her, even after they were married and I had come along. They would turn on the radio in the kitchen and Daddy would grab her—oh how she would laugh—and they would start dancing, almost like they forgot I was in the room. I liked it though; loved to watch them. Sometimes they would pick me up between them and dance with me in the middle. I have some great memories of that time. One of the reasons I love jazz and the blues is because, if I close my eyes while listening to it, I can almost feel their arms around me. Makes them feel close by."

Rudy didn't have those kinds of memories. His daddy had left when he was just a toddler, and he couldn't remember a time when his mother sounded as happy has Frederick's momma must have been. Rudy didn't remember what it was like to have his daddy's arms around him—maybe his daddy had never held him in the same way Frederick's daddy did. He wouldn't be surprised since his daddy had up and left them just like that. Frederick's voice brought Rudy back to the story.

"My momma used to take in laundry. She would rub her hands raw. We didn't have any new fangled washing machines like you see today. In those days, she had to rub everything on a washboard; sometimes, scrape her own skin clean off. Then she would stand over a hot iron, pressing everything perfectly. My momma was a perfectionist; built a fine reputation. The white folks would bring their laundry to her. You can bet that my own shirts were pressed and clean when I went to school. I was one of the cleanest and neatest kids there, even if I didn't have many new clothes. Got a lot of hand-me-downs from the white folks that momma worked for, sometimes through our church too. It didn't pay much, and it was hard work. We didn't have air-conditioning, and summer in the South is not only hot like it gets here but also humid and sticky. The air is thick like molasses. The mosquitoes alone could drive you crazy; they were huge. It felt like you could lasso one and hitch a ride on its back. Yes, sir, they loved the wet, sticky air that was so sweet with the scent of jasmine. Why you could make a million dollars if you could just bottle the smell of the summer night air. In southern California, we have what you call a dry heat. In the South, you just stand still and you're sweating. It can be unbearable. But my momma never complained. She was proud that she was able to contribute to the household income and even put a bit of money aside. Not a lot, mind you, but maybe money to buy me a new suit for Sundays or new shoes. They always thought about me. Just like your momma, Rudy, always thinking about you. She's a hard worker too, wants to be able to put food on the table. Give you what you need."

But what about what I want? Rudy thought as he swatted away a fly.

"Didn't always get what I wanted," Frederick said as though reading Rudy's mind, "but I always had what I needed." Rudy wasn't sure that that was enough for him.

"We stayed out of people's business, followed the rules, worked hard, and life was overall good until the summer I was twelve—just about your age. Things changed that year."

Frederick's expression sobered. This happy-go-lucky man became serious, sad, then almost looked like he could cry. His voice was different; it was lower, as if someone might hear what he was about to say. He paused and Rudy waited, not knowing if he should say something or not. Rudy leaned forward. The sounds of the birds filled his ears. Finally, Frederick continued.

"Rudy, you have to forgive my emotion, but my daddy was the best man I ever knew. He was a fine, hardworking, decent man. He loved me, loved my momma, and loved God. Don't find too many men around like him anymore. He turned the other cheek when people called him names or treated him like a common animal. You know that saying, 'Sticks and stones?' Well, you might think he was weak to take that kind of abuse, but my daddy was smart; knew how to keep his family safe. He knew the truth, so whatever those self-righteous and ignorant people had to say just didn't matter to him. Oh, I suppose it did down deep, but he never let it show. He had pride and self-respect. He didn't like the way he was treated, but it was more important to ensure his family stayed safe. Sometimes bearing your burden silently is the greatest courage there is. He was a fine example of what a man should be."

Reaching out, Frederick put his rough hand on Rudy's shoulder and looked him square in the eye. "I know your daddy left you when you were a little boy, and that's why I want you to hear about my daddy, so that you know there were and are good men in the world—sometimes they're just not that easy to spot. I just hope I have done him proud. You see, Rudy, even as an old man with my daddy in the grave more years than your momma's been alive, I am still his son and want him to be proud of the man I have become. You will want your momma's approval too one day. As far as your daddy is concerned . . . well, he missed the chance to raise a fine boy. You have every right to be disappointed in that. Just don't let your anger toward him define who you are and what you can become."

Rudy was uncomfortable and surprisingly overwhelmed. He didn't know what to say, so he said nothing. In a way, he felt exposed, like Frederick knew how angry he was at his father for leaving him and his mama. But in another weird way, he felt like he had just had his first man-to-man talk, and he kind of liked it. He couldn't talk to his mama about his daddy. Somehow, Frederick seemed to get how he was feeling and was saying it was okay.

Frederick released Rudy's shoulder and drew back his hand. "Well, my daddy worked hard. He worked in a lumber mill. Made a quarter of what a white man would get for the same job. It was hard work—manual labor, just like what you are doing here in this garden. Had to use muscle, sweat, like you pulling out that fence. I remember him coming home, sweaty and smelly with all kinds of aches and pains, sore shoulders, bad back. Still, my daddy did not make waves. He had a good job, was good at it, and just wanted to have a happy life; grow old with his wife and see his son educated and with a life of his own.

"One day, the owner of the mill came to town with his family and wanted to look around; you know, check things out and make sure people were doing what they were supposed to be doing. Seems they were on their way to see some relatives and stopped into town for a few days. The owner was what you would call affluent. Do you know what that means?"

Rudy wasn't sure and shrugged. His grades in school weren't all that great. His heart wasn't in it. He just somehow didn't see the point of school, didn't see how Hemingway and algebra were going to get him out of this hell hole of a neighborhood he was living in.

"Affluent means well-to-do, upper class, rich. He was an important man. Seems like when you have lots of money, you have lots more friends than when you are poor. The man was well connected too, known in town. Might be like Donald Trump coming to town today. Jacob would call him 'Mr. Big Shot Mill Owner.'" Frederick stopped and smiled at Rudy.

"Now this particular day, the owner stopped by the mill with his wife and daughter; wanted to show off. As they were touring the mill, the daughter, who was about eighteen years old, started staring at my daddy, smiling a little. My daddy was a big, strong handsome man in his mid-thirties by then. Had lots of muscles from the long days he put in, sometimes twelve to fifteen hours a day. It was backbreaking work, but he never complained. No, he didn't. But, he was embarrassed by this girl's attention and didn't want any trouble. He just nodded his head in greeting and looked away. It turned out that when they walked by she dropped a pretty kerchief she had worn over her head when they were driving. My daddy saw it and didn't want anyone to think he was going to keep it, so he went after her to return it. He gave it back to her when her daddy was talking business with the mill management. The daughter was mighty friendly, smiling and laughing, saying how grateful she was. I expect the mill owner didn't like my daddy talking to his darling daughter, especially behind his back. He got the idea that my daddy was up to no good. Well, one thing you need to understand was that in those days, it was inconceivable that a white girl would ever flirt with a black man; it was unthinkable that any white girl would want to. It was against every societal rule; in some churches, it was against their religion. Can you imagine bringing God into that warped way of thinking? Well, this girl's papa saw my daddy smiling back at her; thought he was singling her out and flirting with her and called him on it—right on the spot, in front of everyone. He was as mad as a junkyard dog and said, 'What you doing, boy, looking at my girl that way?'"

"I can imagine my daddy was scared, but he looked that man in the eyes and told him that he was just returning the scarf that she dropped and that she was thanking him, though no thanks were needed. You could see the hatred in this man's eyes. He did not like my daddy smiling at his daughter or insinuating that his daughter would be thanking him for anything. After all, his daughter was no nigger lover. I'm sorry to use that word, Rudy. It's a degrading word, but it's what the man said, and I want you to understand how ignorant this man was."

Rudy was unaffected by the word. He'd heard it often enough. It was even used in some of the songs on the radio. He didn't quite get why Frederick was so upset using it but said nothing. His mother had the same reaction one day when the word slipped out, and she had forbidden him from ever using that word again.

"Well, nothing happened that day. He came home and told momma about it. Thought he had dodged a bullet.

"Little did they know that the next morning was my daddy's last day on earth—last time to hold my momma, last time he rubbed my head and kissed my cheek before I went off to school. See, I didn't know what had happened at the mill, and if I had, I'm not sure I could have foreseen the repercussions from that single meaningless event. Funny thing about death . . . it doesn't always give you a warning that it's coming. Sometimes with illness you get an inkling, but that morning was just like any other day to me; just a dab of coolness before the heat came down on us like a wet blanket, the birds singing, just like you hear them now—a day just like any other day. How many times since I have wished I would have hugged my daddy good-bye that morning and told him that I loved him. But I didn't. Didn't know I would never hear his voice humming again in the kitchen, never see him and momma dancing to the radio, never hear his booming voice proclaiming 'Amen' in church anymore. I learned a big lesson that day, Rudy. Not once did I ever take my momma for granted one day of her life after that. You remember that with your mama; she's a real fine woman. She wants to see you grow up to be a fine man. You remember that." Rudy just nodded, wanting to hear the rest of the story, afraid of the words that were coming but drawn in by the cadence of Frederick's voice.

"That next day when my daddy went into work, the head man asked him to come to the office after work; seems they had to get something straight. My daddy was scared but knew he hadn't done anything wrong. His friend and coworker Moses waited for him over by his car. He used to pick up Daddy every morning on his way to the mill and then drive him home. Moses could see that things were going bad. The mill owner arrived as well as some of the most powerful men in town. One of them told Moses he best leave if he knew what was good for him. Moses was a good friend, but he got scared and knew bad things were going to happen. He got in his car, drove it a mile away, hid his car in the woods, and then made his way back to the mill on foot and hid in the bushes. He said he'd never run so hard, like the devil was chasing him. Instead, the devil was waiting for him back at the mill. By the time he got back, it was well past dark. He heard my daddy screaming and crying, begging for mercy, as he approached. He heard loud, angry voices yelling back. He couldn't make out what they were saying, but within minutes, Moses saw them taking my daddy, who was clearly injured, out into the woods. His hands were tied behind his back. They weren't through with him yet. Well, Rudy, you've probably guessed that they killed my daddy."

Frederick paused and took a deep breath. Rudy noticed how quiet it had become; the birds had gone off for their afternoon nap, as Jacob would say.

"I haven't spoken about this in years," he said, "not since I told Yoshito and Jacob many, many years ago."

Rudy felt uncomfortable but couldn't help but feel so sorry for this old man. It seemed to him that the memories were coming back just like they were yesterday.

"How'd he die?" Rudy asked. "Did they shoot him?" Rudy had seen violence on TV and too many news stories of what happened in neighborhoods not far from them, shootings with guns almost every day of the week.

Frederick knew that guns were his only frame of reference. Somehow, shooting someone seemed more humane than what he was about to reveal. Anyone could pick up a gun and shoot. It was a cold and unemotional way to kill someone—no feeling. What happened to his daddy took real hatred, a kind of sick, sadistic evil. It took someone who enjoyed watching another human being struggle for air in the most gruesome way and was willing to use their muscle to kick away a chair out from under a man. Rudy was looking intently at him. Frederick hesitated, but then thought that maybe this boy needed to know what gang or mob mentality could do. He drew in a breath and continued.

"No, Rudy, they lynched him; hung him from a tree in the woods."

Again Frederick paused. It hurt just to say the words, even after all these years. His face was contorted with emotion and recall.

Rudy was stunned and looked at Frederick with wide eyes; in a flash of understanding, the innocence gone. The little bit that he paid attention to at church began to resonate. There was wickedness in the world. People had a choice. Thou shalt not kill. This evil act proved to Rudy the existence of the devil and the home he called hell. For certainly the people that did this to Frederick's daddy ended up in that place. It had been a merciless, inhumane way to die—one he wouldn't inflict on an animal—and it had happened to Frederick's daddy. Then, for a second, Rudy thought of the boy on the ground crying, and realized that this is what happens when people hate.

In an instant, emotions that Rudy couldn't control rose up from his depths, like a geyser reaching the surface: rage at his father for leaving, fury at what had happened to Frederick's father, anger at his friends for turning what he considered harmless mischief into violence, and finally utter disappointment with himself for doing nothing that night in the park. He was shaking and almost crying. Rudy got up and began pacing like a restless animal.

"But he didn't do anything wrong!" Rudy realized he didn't know if he was talking about Frederick's daddy or the boy in the park or himself for being abandoned. But he gathered himself and directed his questions to Frederick. "Couldn't you get help? Call the police? How could Moses just do nothing but watch it happen?" *He was no better than Moses*, he thought.

It seemed Mr. Talkative finally had something to say. Frederick could see that this quiet boy was angry and had walls that ran as deep as the fence in Jacob's yard. There was more going on than his story. Still, Frederick was relieved to see a reaction, despite the extreme emotion. Satisfied that there was hope for this boy, Frederick began comforting him.

"Rudy, Rudy . . . ," Frederick began slowly and deliberately, reaching out to him with one hand and patting the bench with the other, motioning for him to sit back down.

"It's not like today. There was no protection for black families. There was no one, no white man or black man that was going to stand up to those powerful white men. The police, the mayor, they were with them or just looked the other way. Figured my daddy must have deserved it. That's how it was at that time. I look around today and know we still have a ways to go, but compared to then, well, it was a different world."

Frederick paused for a moment, wondering what he could say to explain.

"We are still very imperfect as human beings, and we're not where we need to be. We can be suspicious of each other's races, religions, and differences, and we have no problem pointing the finger at other groups for things gone wrong. But, we've traveled a thousand miles since I was a boy in the South. Next time you think things are unfair, take a look at history and see how far we've come. We'll get to where we need to be if boys like you grow up to be smart, productive citizens and good men."

Rudy was barely listening, still fixated and horrified by what they did to Frederick's daddy and ashamed of himself. Calming down a bit, he sat back down, shaking his head. Could he be a good man, in this time and place, in this neighborhood? He honestly didn't know—not after what had happened in the park.

Finally, Rudy asked, "How'd you find out about your daddy?"

"Moses, God bless him, cut my daddy down as soon as the men left. Could have been there with him if he got caught. He shimmied up the tree and climbed out onto the branch and with a pocket knife, cut the rope that had cut short my daddy's life. Moses was a strong man, but my daddy was big. Do you know he slung my daddy over his shoulders and carried him a mile back to his car, crying and praying the entire time? I don't know how he did it, but he did. Then he drove over to our house after picking up our church reverend.

"Momma had been anxious all night long waiting for my daddy to get home. Then I saw momma's expression when Moses and Reverend Robinson knocked on our screen door. 'Lilly, can we talk to you alone out here on the porch?' they said looking over at me.

"Momma just looked at me blankly and told me to go to my room, and she stepped outside. No one had to tell me that something was terribly wrong. Then I became nervous and anxious. Where was my daddy? Why wasn't he home yet? It was late.

"It wasn't long until I heard my momma's sobbing, and then I knew. Daddy was dead. I just knew it. All three of them told me what happened together. I cried and cried along with my momma. I wanted to yell and scream, but I knew I had to be strong. The undertaker fixed my daddy up for the services as well as he could, covered up what he could. Clothes hid the rest, especially the mark around his neck. I don't know how we made it through the burial services, and then we never talked about it again. It was just too horrible, too grisly. Of course, after time passed, Momma and I would mention Daddy; easy things like, 'Daddy sure would have loved your berry pie tonight, Momma," or she would tell me, 'You're getting to be as strong as your daddy,' or 'Your daddy would be so proud of you,' when I graduated from high school.

"My daddy died on August 24, 1943. Not a word ever appeared in the papers about what happened. It was as if my daddy's life wasn't even worth a footnote."

With that, Frederick and Rudy sat in silence as the heat of the day seemed to lessen and the light seemed to change.

Rudy, now composed, said, "I'm sorry about your daddy, Frederick. He sounds like he was a great man."

Frederick just nodded.

"I think that's enough for today, Rudy. I'll tell Jacob I held you up a bit today. Come back tomorrow, okay?" and with that Frederick got up and walked back through the yard until Rudy heard his back screen door slam.

Chapter 6

Rudy showed up the next day on time, and the next, but did not see Frederick again for the next ten days. Rudy had thought a lot about that story and how Moses had run in fear. In the end, Moses did the right thing and was a good friend. Rudy wanted to do the right thing too—just didn't know how.

Finally, almost two weeks after he had shared his history, Frederick strolled over with Yoshito, picnic basket in hand, and joined Jacob and Rudy.

"What's this?" asked Jacob. "Are we having a party? What's the occasion?"

"No occasion. We just wanted to break bread with friends," Yoshito responded smiling and slightly bowing to Jacob and Rudy.

"Did your flowers tell you to have a picnic?" Jacob asked winking at Rudy. Together, Jacob and Rudy had been making an effort to have a more civil relationship, and he liked it when Jacob got into his playful mood. Jacob had told Rudy about Yoshito hearing his plants talk to him, and Rudy couldn't help but smile at Jacob's teasing. One day while they were working together in the garden, Jacob confessed, "As much as I would like to believe my dear friend is merely insane, I have known Yoshito too long and too well to believe he could be doing anything but telling the truth. Yoshito is one of the most spiritual, gentle souls I have ever met, and if he tells me that the plants are reading recipes in Hebrew, I am afraid that secretly I am going to believe him." Jacob wished some of Yoshito's inner peace would rub off on him.

"Well, let's see what feast you have rendered," Jacob motioned for all to gather at an old wooden table nearby. There was corned beef, fresh Kaiser rolls, mustard, chips, and some sort of a cold noodle salad with carrots and cabbage that Yoshito had made.

"What kind of salad is that?" Rudy asked.

"This is *soba* salad, and I brought it in a *bento* box. This is your first lesson in Japanese," Yoshito replied with a smile. Rudy looked over at the highly lacquered box containing the salad.

After everything was set out, Frederick directed everyone, "Dig in." Everyone reached for a fork except for Yoshito, who produced some chopsticks. When Rudy looked at him, Yoshito held them up and said, "*Hashi.*" Rudy nodded; "*Hashi,*" he repeated.

"You are a fast learner," Yoshito said. Rudy was surprised by his comment; he had never been good at learning anything.

"Wait," Jacob said. "Your gods have not seen fit to furnish this feast with its sweet libation, their golden nectar? What kind of gods are they?" he asked good-naturedly.

"Ah, you're right, Jacob. I left the pitcher on the counter. I'll be right back."

After Frederick left, Rudy told the others, "Frederick told me about his daddy." Yoshito and Jacob looked at him and then at each other.

"Yes, it's a very sad tale. But you must remember, Rudy, it's not just a made-up story. This is Frederick's and his father's story that we are talking about and must be treated with great respect and honor. You must not disgrace the memory by telling your friends casually as you would discuss a football game," said Yoshito. He continued. "If you share the story, it must be done with great reverence, and with Frederick's permission."

"I haven't told anyone. I just got really mad when he told me what happened. Frederick seems so nice, so calm. He must have a lot of anger deep inside just bubbling to get out. I know I would."

This was the most Jacob had heard Rudy talk and was relieved in an odd way.

"Anger gets you nowhere, Rudy. Frederick, Jacob, and I all have reasons to be angry, to want to get even. Sometime this summer, we may all share our stories with you." Jacob glared at Yoshito even as he said this. Surely Yoshito knew he may not want to talk about his past, how hard it was for him.

Yoshito continued. "You may even have a reason to be angry. Anger is like a boomerang. Even though you aim it at someone else, it always comes back to you. It eats you up instead. The greatest peace you can find is to release the anger, and to do so usually requires great courage and forgiveness. Mahatma Gandhi said that, 'The weak can never forgive. Forgiveness is an attribute of the strong.' Sometimes it takes years to get to that place, sometimes decades. One must come to a great understanding and attain great compassion to forgive others." Yoshito had begun speaking to Rudy but finished by aiming his words at Jacob.

Frederick, who had been standing nearby, sat down and joined the conversation. "You want to know how I got past the anger and the fear, Rudy? It took me decades. I started out the other day asking you if you ever heard of the civil rights movement. That was a big part of my healing, and so was meeting my wife, Estelle, who helped me out of the darkness. In the years following my father's murder, I became quiet, introverted, kind of a loner, and was angry inside, but I didn't want any trouble, didn't want to draw any kind of attention to myself. I also made myself a promise that I was going to get my momma and me out of that godforsaken place if it was the last thing I did. I directed my energies on school and became an honor student, and I worked however many jobs it would take to get me through college. I was a teacher—I'll bet you didn't know that about me, did you, Rudy? Taught high school English and literature for thirty five years."

"You were a teacher?" Rudy asked incredulously. Frederick, a teacher and married? There were a lot of surprises about Frederick. Rudy thought he had him sized up as just an old man with a garden; now it felt a bit funny to him that he would be sitting having lunch with a teacher.

"Yes, sir, and I loved every day of it. Each day, I had a chance to mold the thinking of young people like you; try to get them to understand that we are all equal, that anyone can be a doctor or a lawyer or a teacher if they want it badly enough, that no one is better or worse than the next guy. I had the chance to show them different perspectives, experiences and different points of view. Reading and literature can do that: open doors, make you see things differently, allow you to get into another person's head, see what makes them tick."

Frederick continued. "Have you ever read *To Kill a Mockingbird?* You're old enough. You tell your momma to get you that book. It will open your eyes; not only validate the story I told you but also show you that there are people like Atticus Finch in the world. I always thought if I had had a son, I would name him Atticus."

Rudy still didn't understand how any of this had kept Frederick sane, from going out and seeking revenge. Why he hadn't exploded with rage?

"I don't understand how all this helped you after . . . ." Rudy looked away, the words fading.

"I was angry for a time, but then came the change—in the world and in me. Now, I know you have heard of Dr. Martin Luther King."

Rudy nodded, of course he had. Frederick must think he didn't know anything.

"Well, I met Dr. King, shook his hand."

Rudy listened wide-eyed. Frederick knew him?

"It was one of the proudest days of my life. I can't say we were personal friends, but one day he came right up to me in a crowd, grabbed my hand, shook it, and thanked me for coming to the marches. It gives me chills to think of it even after all these years.

Imagine you meeting the President of the United States. It was like that.

"He started the change. He was what you would call a catalyst of change. He altered the trajectory not just of the black man but of all men. He was there at the beginning, helping change come. I used to go and listen to him speak, met Estelle at one of the rallies. Oh, you would have liked her. She was a wonderful woman; got me back on track, found a softness inside of me again."

Frederick paused and seemed to suddenly travel to a place only he could see. A smile crossed his face. Rudy wished he could see what his mind was seeing. Coming back from that long time ago, Frederick continued.

"Soon after the first time I heard him, I started marching with him. Do you know what I found out? There were white people walking with me—sometimes arm in arm. They weren't all like the mill owner. I discovered that there were a lot of people who were now brave enough to come forward and say things were wrong. Black people started to stand up and say, 'I'm not sitting in the back of the bus anymore,' 'I'm going to go to the same school as white kids,' 'I'm going to sit at a counter in a restaurant and expect service,' and governments were starting to listen. Jack and Bobby Kennedy made changes along with Dr. King. That was quite a team, but of course, we know what happened to them.

"Those years were some of the most hopeful and exhilarating; you could feel changes happening while you lived it. Have you ever seen one of those time-elapsed movies where you see a flower opening up, or the seasons changing over a landscape? Well, that's what it was like for all of us who lived during that time. Everything seemed to be happening fast, and we were watching history before our very eyes. Yes, sir. Now this might sound like a contradiction, but sometimes in the moment, it didn't seem so fast. When we heard about the deaths of Jack Kennedy, then Dr. King, and finally Bobby Kennedy . . . well, it just about took the wind out of our sails. So much tragedy, but I guess they completed the work the good Lord had in mind. Things were never the same again—in a good way. Yes, I'd have to say that those men accomplished their mission."

Sighing deeply, he continued. "We're not perfect yet, Rudy—lots of intolerance from lots of people—but at least now we know it is wrong."

Rudy thought about his friends who thought everyone was inferior, below them. Maybe he had begun to think that way too, but now it wasn't so clear. He didn't think that way anymore—not after hearing Frederick's tale, not after the park. Then he thought, *Look at me. I'm having lunch with a Jew, an Asian, and a black man.* He looked at these men gathered around this table and thought they were nice and not much different from him. They were older, of course, but they seemed to get it. He was beginning to like being with them, being included in their conversations. They were interesting, but they were also kind and respected each other despite their differences. Rudy's friends would freak.

Frederick interrupted his thoughts, continuing. "I suppose my daddy's death was just one example of the injustice those three men were fighting against. I see my daddy as being part of the struggle and coming out the victor, not that rich, white mill owner. During that time, listening to Dr. King and his message, I came to a reconcilement of what happened; not approval, not acquiescence, not apathy, mind you—never those things. Oh, I can tell you that at one time or another I did feel hatred, wanted to take revenge, considered violence, and had such deep sorrow, but I wanted desperately to be better than those men that killed my daddy. I did not want to become one of them. I wanted to be an instrument for good. God knows I'd seen enough evil in this world. So I prayed and prayed, and He heard me. At some point, a deeper understanding of humanity's weaknesses and fears took hold, and I was able to turn that energy into something positive. I wanted to make a difference in the next generations' lives through teaching, and I hope I influenced the young people in my classes. I did my best."

With that, everyone was silent. Rudy sat there a bit uneasy, processing everything he had heard. Jacob seemed uncomfortable too, but Yoshito had that peaceful look of understanding written across his face.

After a time, Rudy asked, "What happened to your wife?"

"Ah, my dear Estelle. You think this garden is beautiful? Estelle would have put those roses over there to shame. She was the light of my life. We were married for thirty-three years. She died six years ago. She was a good woman; kept me sane and positive when I was down, encouraged me to work in the garden, and didn't think I was crazy when I told her I heard my ancestors singing. Well, maybe at first she did, but when she saw I was serious, she just told me to get out in the garden and lift my voice with theirs and make a beautiful noise to heaven!" Frederick looked at Rudy, his seriousness turning to a smile.

"And there was no one, and I mean no one, who could make an apple rhubarb pie like her. Remember, fellas?" he asked, looking at Jacob and Yoshito for confirmation.

"You knew Estelle?" Rudy asked, somehow being surprised and feeling a bit left out.

Jacob and Yoshito nodded, smiling to themselves.

"Estelle was a wonderful woman. She could cook like you wouldn't believe. Had us over for the holidays all the time—any excuse to feed us," Jacob replied, smiling at Frederick.

"She and my wife, Grace, were very close. We always thought Estelle was very elegant," Yoshito added.

Yoshito was married too? Rudy thought. He wondered about any surprise Jacob might have.

"Grace was a beautiful woman. Her name suited her," Frederick added gently.

Yoshito nodded, and for the first time, Rudy thought he saw tears in Yoshito's eyes. Seeing Rudy looking at him, Yoshito said, "I will tell you about Grace one day but not today. Today we must get back to work. My plants are waiting for me to satiate their thirst, and I can see you are making good progress on pulling down the fence." Yoshito moved to get up.

"Well, here we go, eh, Rudy? Are you finished eating?" Jacob asked.

"Sure, thanks for lunch. It was really good."

"*Domo arigatou gozaimasu.* That means thank you very much," Yoshito replied with a slight bow.

"Come on, Rudy. Frederick returns to his singing, and Yoshito seeks better conversation with the ferns. Our work waits for no one but us," Jacob said as he hoisted his body from the chair.

And so together they continued to pull down the fence inch by inch.

Chapter 7

Rudy let the screen door slam behind him when he went home that night, the same as he did every night.

"Rudy! How many times do I need to ask you not to slam doors around here?" Rudy's mother stepped out from the kitchen to see her son walking past.

"Sorry, Mama."

"How's that fence coming?" She was hesitant to ask about it after all the fights they had had about him taking that job, but it had been several weeks now and she had to know. How he had resisted. She absolutely knew that she needed to get him away from those boys he had been hanging out with before school ended. They were up to no good; she could feel it in her bones.

"It's okay." That was a better response than she was expecting from her quiet and resistant son. How she worried about him, especially at this age, with no father figure to guide him.

She considered herself a good Christian woman, but lately, now that Rudy was becoming a teenager, she began to feel the same anger toward Rudy's father that she had felt when he first left. This boy needed his father, although she was entirely sure that he would not be the role model she had believed him to be when she met and married him. How he had swept her off her feet with his sweet talking; "baby" this and "sweetheart" that. He was a big talker too. Made grandiose plans that she hung her hat on that never amounted to anything. He just liked to have fun, keep everything light, everybody laughing. She had loved that about him in the beginning.

But everything changed when she unexpectedly became pregnant. He became distant, stayed out and drank. He stuck it out for a while, and then one day, he was gone. Just like that. She didn't have to wonder why. He had no patience for a baby or toddler and hated feeling weighed down with the responsibilities of fatherhood. How she could curse him! She didn't even know if he was alive or dead after he moved away. He never bothered to keep in touch with his own flesh and blood. What kind of a man could just walk away like that?

She couldn't count the number of times she had gotten down on her knees and begged the Lord to watch over and protect her son from bad influences, to make him a better man than his father. Yet, she wondered if it was possible with no examples to show him the way.

"Frederick and Jacob, are they nice, treating you okay?" she pushed.

"Yeah, they're . . . they're nice. Yoshito, too."

Rudy's mama was more than satisfied with that answer. The fights appeared to be over. She breathed a sigh of relief to herself.

Reluctantly she added, "Those boys were over here looking for you again today. I keep telling them you have a summer job, but they seem persistent." She hated telling him. She didn't want him to hang around with those kids, but she knew he would find out directly from them. "Said they would be over at the park tonight. I don't think you should go out tonight, Rudy. Those boys are bound to be looking for trouble."

"That's okay. I think I'll stay home. I don't feel like going out tonight," Rudy replied. He couldn't go back to the park and couldn't tell his mama why.

Rudy's mama tried to control her shock. She had been waiting for an argument. Concerned, she asked, "You feeling okay? Everything all right?"

"Yeah, I'm just tired tonight. I worked really hard today, Mama." That at least was the truth, even if it wasn't the entire reason. But he had dug out five feet of fence today—a new record for him—and he felt it in muscles he didn't even know he had.

"Okay, Rudy. Well, go take a shower, and I'll have some dinner for you when you get out."

"Okay." Rudy began walking in the direction of his room but stopped as he was turning the corner into the hallway. "Mama? You ever heard of a book called Killing Mockingbirds?"

"You mean, *To Kill a Mockingbird*?" she asked confused. "Yes, I read it in high school. Why?"

"Just thought I might like to try to read it. Frederick mentioned it. No big deal."

"I'll pick up a copy at the library tomorrow. Now go on and take your shower."

Rudy's mama stared at the doorway where her son had stood a minute ago. She didn't know what was happening to her son, where the combative young man had gone, and now he wanted to read for fun, out of curiosity? Whatever was happening, she liked it, and yes, it was a very big deal.

Chapter 8

The first month of summer had come and gone and nearly half of the fence was out. The work had seemed so hard at first, that fence fighting Rudy like a warrior. He didn't know if he was getting stronger or just used to the job, but things seemed a bit easier. He was getting along with everyone better now too, although that Jacob was one tough old guy. On this particular day, Rudy showed up to find Jacob waiting for him.

"You have a reprieve today, my young Goliath. Yoshito needs some assistance with a new project in his garden. Do you think you are up for a bit of a change today?" Jacob asked.

"Sure, not a problem," Rudy said, grateful to have something new to do. Pulling out that fence was strenuous work, and he was sure this new project would be too if they needed his help, but at least it was something different.

"Very good. Maybe if you are lucky, you will hear Yoshito's plants talking up a storm," Jacob replied straight-faced but in good humor.

"Go ahead and go over to his house. Maybe I'll be by later, or maybe just see you tomorrow. We'll see how this old body feels as the day goes along." Jacob waved Rudy off with his hand.

"Okay. See ya, Jacob," Rudy said as he walked down the driveway, not yet wanting to climb over the drooping fence through Frederick's yard to Yoshito's.

Heading toward the street, he realized as he did nearly every day that he left Jacob's, what a difference there was between the drab street scene as compared to the life, greenery, and color in these three backyards. He looked more closely at the homes now, with new eyes. Mostly clean, but a bit run down; the paint was chipping off some, new roofs were needed on others that could not be afforded, metal screen doors needed to protect the inside from the outside. Then there was the house with the cars on the lawn. Everyone in the neighborhood knew it was a crack house, even the police knew—they were there often enough—yet nothing seemed to change. The people going in and out were not people you'd want to cross. He lived up around the corner and knew his mother hated her small house that needed more repairs than they had money.

Funny, but Rudy felt freer being outside than he had before he started to work in the garden. He felt privileged in a way—like he was in on a secret. He'd told his mama that the backyard was unbelievable, beautiful beyond what could be imagined. Unless you had been in it, smelled the air, heard the birds, seen the color and the abundance, he didn't think she could comprehend the beauty hidden behind those three nondescript houses.

Rudy had even come to love the feel of mulched soil running through his fingers. He was learning a lot too. Before this summer, he would not have known the difference between a perennial and an annual. He never knew some flowers grew from a bulb, and he certainly could have never imagined how much he would enjoy watching vegetables grow. Sometimes Frederick would call him away from the fence to assist in preparing a bed for a new vegetable, feeding ones already on their way to maturity, or tying up tomato or bean plants that were getting big and gangly and having a mind of their own. It was actually fun.

Still, Rudy had said nothing to his friends about it. They knew he had a summer job during the day that his mama had fixed up through church, but they had no idea what he was doing. He didn't want them to know, didn't want them putting down Jacob, Frederick, and Yoshito, and didn't want them making fun of him. Truthfully, he rarely saw them anymore; they had lost their appeal. Rudy was beginning to understand that they were narrow-minded and their beliefs too closely resembled those of the people that killed Frederick's daddy. He saw that more clearly now that he had been away from them working for Jacob. If they asked him to go out at night, maybe pull another shoplift, he just told them he couldn't; he said he had to get up early or his mama needed him for something. Rudy was sure that they were saying bad things about him, but it didn't seem to matter as much as it used to—he just wasn't interested in that kind of trouble anymore, kind of like Frederick's daddy. He liked imagining himself like Frederick's daddy; maybe because he didn't have a father of his own, or maybe he was just growing up. Even Jacob, Frederick, and Yoshito had turned out to be nicer—cooler—than he thought they would be. Jacob was a bit more aloof, but each of them treated him like he was special, like they had all come to like him. They treated him like he was one of them, and he liked it. It was a funny turn of events, but he couldn't spend any more time wondering about it.

As Rudy walked up Yoshito's drive and entered his backyard, he could now see up close what he had only seen from Jacob's backyard two doors away. Yoshito's garden had an entirely different feel than Jacob's. Both were wonderful, but Yoshito's felt almost like going into a church. It was very peaceful and quiet, very shaded, the prominent sound coming from water running through bamboo into a hollowed-out stone spilling into small pebbles underneath. Around the stone basin, there were lush, low trees and ferns of every variety. At an elevated level farther back, Rudy saw some kind of gazebo. He wondered what it was for.

The back screen door slammed behind Yoshito as he came out of the house and walked over to where Rudy stood. Rudy wondered if his mother would scold Yoshito as she did him.

A gray and white stocky cat followed Yoshito and then cautiously approached Rudy to sniff his pant leg and investigate this new visitor. Rudy stood still, and as the cat deemed him safe, began to rub against his jeans, moving in figure eights in and out between his legs. "Hey boy," Rudy said gently as he bent over to pet what was becoming a new friend. In response, the cat purred loudly, arching his back to meet Rudy's hand.

"Rudy, this is Ling; Ling, this is Rudy," Yoshito said smiling, enjoying watching a new softness flow out of Rudy. "Ling has a very keen sense of people. He must find your spirit to be a gentle one."

Rudy smiled and stood, enjoying being described as gentle. "This is the first time I've seen your garden up close. It's so peaceful and restful, really beautiful."

"Thank you. It is in this space that I let go of the worries of this world and where I dream of the next. You are too young to think of such things yet, but as you get older, you begin to wonder about the place where you will spend eternity." He smiled at Rudy and then continued. "Let me give you a tour before we give ourselves over to our project for the day." Rudy followed Yoshito down the path toward the flowing water.

"You will find that while my garden is harmonious with Frederick's and Jacob's gardens, it has certain elements from my culture that you will not find in the others. First, you will notice this stone mosaic path. You can see the shape of the stones and the manner in which they are laid gives an illusion of movement, as if a river was flowing and leading us toward the water source." Stepping closer to the rustic stone bowl, he continued. "This type of water basin is called a *tsukubai*. Can you say that?"

Rudy attempted to mimic Yoshito. "*Tsukubai.*"

"Yes, that's it. The *tsukubai* is known as a crouching basin. In order to use it, one must adopt a position of humility. One must remember that he is only a small part of the world, not the world itself. You will see the larger and smaller pebbles surrounding it in a definite pattern. This is all part of the desired arrangement. I have devised the water to flow like a fountain so one can always hear the sound of trickling water. Behind it and to the side is a stone lantern called *ishi toro,* which contains the three basic shapes, the square, the circle and the triangle. Long ago, lanterns would be lit to provide lighting for tea ceremonies that took place after dark or first thing in the early morning hours. I will occasionally put a candle out here, but I am afraid I have adopted technology by using electrical lighting for night time. It highlights this area very nicely."

Walking along pathways of stone, Rudy noticed that most all the plantings were evergreen. Here and there was a splash of color, and he was proud that he could identify many by their names, like the Japanese maple and hydrangeas, the orchids he saw in pots situated at random, the long iris leaves, and the azaleas and camellia bushes that in late winter and early spring would provide some color. Mostly though, there was this carpet of green textures—mosses, grasses, trees, ferns, bushes—everything lush. As they worked their way along an upward path, they approached the wood gazebo that Rudy had noticed earlier.

"What is that?" Rudy questioned, pointing to the small retreat.

In the corner of the yard, a bit elevated, was a small structure surrounded by maple trees. Its four corner posts and the cross beams were in dark wood with open walls and bamboo covering the roof. The floor was large, flat stones with some color; maybe slate with bamboo mats thrown about. It was a simple but serene place. Rudy felt like whispering as if it was a holy place and he was on hallowed ground.

"This is where I come to meditate, to pray . . . where I come to open my mind to positive experience and energy. See how the sunlight is filtered through the delicate leaves of the maple? It is a beautiful setting. I come here to gain strength each day to face the hardships of life and to forgive past wrongs and prepare myself for my existence on the next plane."

"Hardships? You seem to have it made here," Rudy said, clearly confused. Yoshito appeared to have a calm existence, didn't seem to have many hardships. What past wrongs was he talking about? Rudy wanted to know.

"Everyone must endure hardships, Rudy; no one is exempt. I think you have already discovered that at a young age. For you it may be not having a father or financial hardships." Rudy almost visibly winced. Yoshito had zeroed in on his greatest pain. "For me, it is the loss of Grace, my wife. I miss her terribly. One does not easily recover from a loss like that. Her loss opened a great space for loneliness and bitterness to take hold. I must work to not let those negative energies move into that space but fill it up with other things." They continued to walk on.

"I must also open my mind to forgiveness to let go of past wrongs. In the Christian tradition, there is a prayer called the Our Father. Do you know it?" Rudy nodded yes, but he hadn't said prayers in a very long time.

"There is a beautiful line that says, 'Forgive us our trespasses, as we forgive those who trespass against us.' I cannot ask the great Creator to forgive me if I cannot forgive others; instead, He will bestow mercy on me to the degree that I have bestowed mercy on others."

"Who do you have to forgive, Yoshito?" Rudy asked cautiously, knowing he was taking liberties in Yoshito's personal business.

"Come, let us begin our work, and I will tell you." Rudy followed Yoshito to an area where there was a small, winding path surrounded by shrubbery. The trail had some kind of plastic looking covering over the ground. To the side were bags and bags of fine gravel.

"You are a strong boy, and I am an old man. I need your muscles to finish this job. Here on the path you will lay the gravel, in small piles every few feet, and then I will smooth them out."

Rudy did as he was told and worked for the next two hours, opening bags, pouring out gravel into even piles around the trail, waiting patiently for Yoshito to tell his story. Yoshito directed him, pointing here and there while crawling on his hands and knees spreading the stones with his glove-covered hands. When Rudy was done, he helped Yoshito spread the stones evenly, the gravel digging into his knees through his jeans. Afterward, Rudy wiped the sweat with his shirttail while Yoshito bid him to sit for a while on a nearby stone and cool down. Instead of joining him, Yoshito grabbed an unusually heavy-looking rake and began raking the stones. Rudy wondered what was going on. Watching Yoshito drag the rake this way and that, he noticed that patterns began to slowly emerge—wavy and winding ridges and furrows gave the illusion of movement, of water. It was art like Rudy had never seen before. He sat mesmerized while Yoshito created a river of stone. It too was headed toward the water basin at the front of the yard. Here and there, Yoshito would stop and pull a wide comb out of his pocket and expertly drag the comb in a circle creating water droplets in the middle of the waves as if this river were caught in a rain shower.

Rudy sat there silently, watching the master move his rake back and forth, and when it was done, Rudy remarked, "It's unbelievable." He could not believe what had been created from small pebbles.

Yoshito smiled and said, "Yes, it is profound that even a seemingly dull, small pebble is really something beautiful by nature." Yoshito put down the rake and joined Rudy in the shade on a nearby rock. "What do you see, Rudy?"

"I see a river heading toward your back door, and it's raining."

"You are a smart boy. How does it make you feel?"

"Relaxed . . . happy . . . cool."

"Me, too. In this chaotic world, we must always look for ways to find peace inside." For a minute, Yoshito seemed to be gathering his thoughts, looking across time and space.

"I promised you a story."

Rudy nodded.

"I do not tell many people this story. It is not of a very happy time for me. But in other ways, it is very dear. I tell you because I trust you, Rudy. I think you are a good boy who will grow up to be a fine man. I think of you as a friend."

Rudy was so touched by this. A friend. He hadn't thought of these men as friends, but if truth be known, he had come to like them despite their age and oddities. He liked being thought of as a friend—Yoshito's friend. Rudy remembered thinking of Yoshito as "the jap" and now regretted thinking of him in such a disrespectful way. This summer hadn't been so bad after all. He had learned so much and found himself changing. He saw things, people differently.

Rudy looking embarrassed, but wanting Yoshito to know he was sincere, said, "I like you too—you, Frederick, and Jacob."

"Never underestimate the power of friendship, Rudy. Aristotle once said that, 'Without friends, no one would choose to live, though he had all other goods.' I think he was right. And so now I will confide my story to you, my friend."

Rudy nodded to Yoshito who seemed to see something far and away out in a distance.

Chapter 9

"Do you remember hearing in your history class about Pearl Harbor being bombed during World War II? It happened on December 7, 1941. It must seem like a long time ago to you, long before you were born. But I was ten years old on that day. My family lived in Salinas, California. We were farmers. My father and mother were *Issei*, born in Japan and came to America as young children. I had an older brother who was twelve and a little sister who was seven. My first ten years were very happy. I did not know then about the anti-Japanese sentiment that had sprung up in the first forty years of the twentieth century, especially in California where 90 percent of Japanese immigrants settled. I did not understand that the world was poised to hate us after December 7. My father and mother were longtime residents, and my brother, sister, and I were born here, were citizens. People only saw the shape of our eyes, heard our name, and wanted to believe we were part of the conspiracy against this, our country. Some people called us a 'dangerous element.'"

Yoshito shook his head, still in disbelief that people could feel that way.

"Like Frederick's experience in the South, there was much discrimination against the Japanese in the early part of the century, especially on the West Coast. In 1905, California passed a law that prohibited marriage between Caucasians and Mongolians, which is a name used to describe Japanese and other East Asians. In San Francisco, they segregated schools in 1906. Ninety-three students were affected and sent to Chinatown to learn. Of those, twenty-five were American citizens. You can see there was much fear and ignorance. It didn't matter that those children were Americans.

"So when the Japanese attacked Pearl Harbor, it was as if we had attacked Pearl Harbor. My father understood right away that there would be trouble. I remember him listening to the radio and telling my mother that we would pay for Japan's actions. My mother did not understand, and neither did I as I sat on the floor playing, listening to them talk. Two months later, on February 19, 1942, the President of the United States, Franklin Roosevelt, authorized the internment of Japanese Americans. Do you understand the term 'internment,' Rudy?"

Rudy had a vague idea of what he was talking about but couldn't articulate it. So he shook his head, almost afraid to hear the words. Yoshito continued.

"The order authorized the military to gather Japanese Americans and hold them in a camp together. While it was frightening and terrible, I think my father was almost relieved that something had happened. We had been waiting for the shoe to drop, and now it had. There had also been reported violence against the Japanese, and now at least we would be together as a family and in a protected area, my father said. There was fear in his voice though. I heard it, and it frightened me a bit as a little boy. I tried to follow my father's lead. If he told us not to worry, that is what I would say to my brother and sister to reassure them when they became scared. 'Just follow directions and nothing bad will happen,' my father would say. We left the care of our farm to our neighbors and friends who were sympathetic and saw the injustice toward our family, toward our race. We also left them our most prized belongings, items handed down through the family. We were afraid looters would come into our home in our absence. Of course, we did not know how long we would be away. Surely this madness was only temporary. Little did we know, we would be gone for three years."

"Three years?! What was it like being forced to move into the camp?" Rudy asked incredulously.

"In April, we were ordered to bring the barest of belongings to the school auditorium. We showed up in our best clothes with one suitcase each, containing clothes, maybe a blanket or some special item. My parents allowed each of us children to take one small toy or something that would give us comfort. My sister took a stuffed bear that she slept with every night. My brother took a deck of cards that we could play with. I took some drawing paper and colored pencils, but in between the pages, I hid a map of California. I had always loved geography, but now, more than ever, I wanted to know where I was going and how far away it was from home. Sometimes I would sit for hours looking at the map, and by the end of the war, it barely held together. It had been handled and opened and closed so many times that there were tears along the folds. I would trace the progress of our trip to the camp, plan our trip home, look for escape routes, and check to see how far we were from the closest town or mountain range. I needed a sense of my space in the world and measured the miles to home." Rudy could feel the emotion and isolation in every word Yoshito said.

"That must have been really hard for a ten-year-old boy," Rudy offered.

Yoshito looked at him. "Yes, it was. It was difficult for all of us. My poor mother worried about us children day and night, and my father worried about what would become of our lives—our future."

Yoshito continued. "That morning at the auditorium, we checked in and we were tagged along with our bags—like we were Christmas presents being delivered. Buses were waiting to take us away to Civilian Assembly Centers. These were holding places or temporary camps until we were moved to our permanent camp, what they called relocation centers. There were two camps in California; one in Manzanar and another in Tule Lake. Manzanar is the most famous and where we spent those years of our confinement. You cannot imagine, Rudy, how terrible it is to be surrounded by barbed wire fences, your personal freedom taken away because of your heritage. We were not spies. That is what happens when fear takes hold—mania takes over."

Rudy thought of his friends who belittled everyone, who wanted to control everything, take what they thought was rightfully theirs. Now that he heard these stories, it seemed like what was happening in his neighborhood and in his school today and that what pervaded his community was based on intolerance and fear.

"Manzanar was in the middle of nowhere. Fifty miles from the Nevada border near Death Valley, about two hundred and twenty miles northeast of where we stand today. Go look for it on a map, and you will see it situated near a city called Independence. Ironic, isn't it, that our internment was just seven miles from a place called Independence?" Yoshito shook his head sadly.

He looked up at the sunshine and continued.

"It was very hot in the summer, very cold in the winter. Desolate, just some leftover groves of trees, remnants of more fertile days of decades past. It was a desert; not like here where everywhere you look you see flowers and bushes and fruit trees. We did maintain a farm for the camp, but other than that, there was not the lush vegetation you see where we live today. What I remember most vividly was the dust and the sand; dust and sand everywhere. The dust storms were horrible, like tiny needles hitting your skin if you were outside. Even inside, the dust seemed to find its way through the cracks in the floorboards, crevices in the walls, and knots in the wood. It would settle in our hair and get into our bedding and clothes. It was everywhere. I think those sandy—brown-colored memories may be one reason why working in this garden has filled me with so much pleasure. It is green and alive. I can make the soil dark and rich with just a little effort on my part. I know my friend Jacob has told you that I hear plants speaking to me, yes?"

Yoshito smiled and Rudy nodded, laughing to himself until Yoshito said, "It is true, Rudy. I do hear my plants speak to me. Oh, not conversation, but sometimes when I come out on a very hot day like to today, I will hear whispered murmuring, saying, 'I'm thirsty.'

Other times when I come out and am watering the plants and the leaves are bobbing up and down, I hear them laughing as if they are crying for joy. It is a great honor that I am able to provide them that happiness and help them achieve their potential, which is to honor the Divine Creator with their great beauty."

Rudy was staring at Yoshito. He could tell he was serious—and he had to admit that he believed him. These were not the ravings of a crazy man. Yoshito was as solid and grounded as they came.

"And I always welcome my plants into Eden and tell them how beautiful they are and how much they will love being here in this space, and I promise them I will be a good caretaker. I think they understand, just the way Ling understands when I talk to him. This garden, what you see, is so opposite of where I spent three very fundamental and life-changing years. I think for many years I felt as spiritually dried up as the hard, impenetrable soil I walked on. Then, as I started nurturing this space, I felt myself being nurtured. It has been very comforting and restorative for me. Do you understand, Rudy?"

Rudy nodded. He really did understand. Something similar was happening to him this summer. Every time he put the shovel in the dirt, or got his hands dirty in the soil working to free the fence from the ground, he felt healthier on the inside and out. In a way, he was proud of his callused hands, as if he had worked to earn a prize. He wanted hands like Jacob, rough, callused, and dry.

Yoshito continued. "Those years were long, and while I remember some individual days and events or particular feelings I had, the rest is bound together in one block of time. I think some things are better not remembered." Yoshito stood up and began to walk toward the house. Rudy didn't know if that would be the end of the story for that day, but then Yoshito looked back at him and said, "Let's go back to the house and have something to drink to cool ourselves. The memories of the heat and dust have made my mouth dry, and like my green friends here, I thirst."

Rudy followed behind Yoshito until they reached some chairs near the back door under a small patio. Yoshito brought out some tea, and Ling came and lay down on the cool stone floor as if readying himself to hear the rest of Yoshito's tale.

"I had slept the last several hours on the bus. As we neared, my mother shook me awake and told me we were almost to our destination. As I cleared my head and looked out the window, I saw a desert wasteland with mountains in the distance and the great Mount Whitney. Our bus then drove through a gate, barbed wire fences on either side of it, into a compound. After collecting our bags, we were led to our tar-papered barracks. Each barrack was broken into many units. Our family had one of these units, with other families in the other units. Each unit was only the size of this patio, Rudy. All of us slept in this room together for the first year and a half. My parents attempted to partition off sleeping space for themselves and for us with a hanging blanket, but some nights it was so cold that the blanket came down to cover us children. We slept on army cots and made makeshift mattresses with straw, and later as our clothes were worn and torn, rags. We were issued two blankets each, but in the winter, with the holes in the floors and walls, they just weren't enough to keep us warm, and often we would sleep in our clothes. The summer, of course, was the opposite problem; it was difficult to keep cool.

"Although I remember having great fear the first year, I think for us children, it was an easier life. Of course we complained about the heat and cold and dust and sand, but on a good day, we would go out and play with other children, even eventually going to school. For my parents, this degradation and humiliation was not as palatable, and they had a fine line to walk of being too friendly with the camp administration and being too vocal about our conditions and treatment.

"The first year was the worst. Much of the work on the camp was incomplete when we arrived. Refrigeration was an issue; plumbing was an issue; there was no privacy, not enough supplies. I remember my sister crying once. When I tried to comfort her she didn't want to tell me what was wrong. Somehow I managed to get her to tell me. She had had to go to the bathroom with a line of women watching her. The women did not have any stalls around the toilets, so there was no privacy, no way to be modest. My mother would take a blanket and try to wrap it around my sister while she completed her business. It was humiliating for my sister, and I imagine for my mother, but if my mother complained to my father, I never heard it.

"There were many other trials that first year. Early in 1943, the government wanted us all to sign a Loyalty Oath to the government stating we would serve in the Armed Forces to defend the United States if ordered; that we had unqualified allegiance to the United States, would defend her against any foreign attacks, and that we would foreswear any allegiance or obedience to Japan. This sparked much controversy in the camp. There were many who felt that if you agreed to the oath, you were traitors. Yet, if you didn't, America would brand you as disloyal, and you could be sent to Tule Lake with other perceived enemies and be separated from your family. There were factions on both sides, angry and ready to fight for their point of view.

"At one point, trouble and dissatisfaction had been growing, and my father heard rumblings. He cautioned us to stay close to our barracks. My father was not a coward or unprincipled, but like Frederick's father, he wanted no trouble and only thought about the welfare of his family. Then one day something happened that ignited the anger—the straw that broke the camel's back. It incited faction leaders to make speeches that fueled the fire, which led to riots by early nightfall. When the speeches began, my father knew that would be the day to get through unharmed, and he and my mother ran to our usual play areas and rounded us up to come home. I almost thought I was in some sort of trouble for not completing a chore satisfactorily or for teasing my sister, as my father seemed so agitated and his grip on my arm was firm and rough, and his steps so fast and strides long, that I had to run next to him to keep up.

"When we got to our barracks, we were told to play indoors with no explanation, as my father paced the floor and my mother sat quietly at the small table with my sister waiting for time to pass. As the afternoon and then evening progressed and the sky deepened, we did not light our oil lamp that night but went to bed uncommonly early with no dinner. Again, no explanation was provided, and before long, no explanation was needed. We heard large groups of people running past our door; they sounded angry. I remember being frightened and my sister crying in my mother's arms as she tried to quiet and comfort her. My brother and I lay in bed shivering, with the blankets up to our chins; our eyes open wide, watching shadows race past our windows. My father's look was all we needed to know that we should not be asking questions but remain quiet. I think it was the time I was most afraid. Not surprisingly, the riots did not have a good ending. Many people were in the hospital with gunshot wounds and two young men died. Such a shame."

Yoshito paused and took a long draught of his tea. Rudy said nothing but waited. Yoshito leaned forward, his elbows on his knees. Ling got up and moved toward him so that his head looked up between Yoshito's legs. He motioned for Ling to sit in his lap, and he obliged, comfortably settling in his lap. As Yoshito stroked Ling's back and then his chin, his face seemed to relax and a look of love settled lightly as he spoke endearments to Ling. Rudy was touched and wanted to console Yoshito the way Ling had. He wanted to do that for his friend.

"After the riots, things settled down into a more comfortable routine. There was a feeling of resignation around camp. While no one should ever be resigned to being captive, it did make for a less stressful life. It took a while for me to be unafraid, but after that first year, as the detainees changed, so did the camp. Things were being repaired and in working order. We started to go to school more regularly with real teachers; supplies were more accessible, and we were given privileges to go outside the gates of camp. We were also able to have more space to ourselves. Once the oaths were signed, people were able to relocate out of the camp to the Midwest or eastern coast if they had sponsors. Families began leaving, and the camps became less congested. Clubs were started, woman were getting their hair done, how-to classes of various hobbies popped up. Don't get me wrong, Rudy, this was no resort. These improvements did not make what happened right or okay and did not balance the damage that was done."

Rudy nodded he understood. Captivity like this was just wrong.

Yoshito continued. "I do believe that as children we could more easily adapt to this new lifestyle than our parents. After all, we didn't understand the magnitude or the cost of what we left behind and didn't know what it had taken to get there in the first place the way my mother and father did. I don't think we understood the depth of the disenfranchisement and humiliation of being imprisoned because of the slant of our eyes, regardless if some of us were U.S. citizens, until we were older and witnessed the toll it took on my parents, read the history books, and finally understood what and why things had happened.

"This injustice and my response to its affects on me and my family is something I have struggled with all my life, Rudy. Many Japanese did not want to leave Manzanar when the order came that we could go home. Understandably, they were fearful of what they might find when they went home. I struggle to forgive the events that made my mother and father afraid to go home and then led us to what came later. It was a long time before things returned to something called normal. Once, when I was a teenager, I remember asking my father if I could go camping with my friend from school. My father looked at me confused, shaking his head, 'What, you want to go to camp?' I told him, 'Camping in the woods with Eric and his family, you know, hiking, fishing?' I could see understanding move across his face, his muscles relax, and the tension ease out of his body. 'It's just a camping trip; it's okay,' I replied. 'Yes, okay,' he said, as he put his hand to his face. I realized then how close that experience, that pain, was to the surface.

"My father never wanted to talk about it once we returned home. As I got older, I had some questions, wanted to discuss what had happened. My father would just calmly tell me, 'That was in the past. There is no point in visiting that place again.' And so whatever pain he still had, he carried it with him to his grave. I always regretted that I could not help relieve him of that burden."

"What happened when you went home?" Rudy wanted to know.

"We were luckier than most. Our neighbors took care of the place, worked the land for the profits during our absence. We had our belongings returned that we had left with them, but it became apparent after two years back that my father's heart was no longer in it. The house had bad memories, so he put the place up for sale, and within six months after that we relocated to Southern California. My father opened a dry cleaning business in the Fairfax district, and we had a good life for many years. It was different from farming, but that was one of the reasons my father liked it. He felt like he was truly starting fresh, and he was good at it. He took great pride in having repeat business and new customers referred to him from his existing customers. He gained a good reputation in the local community."

"What happened to your brother and sister?" Rudy asked.

"Ah, that is more difficult. My brother never quite recovered from Manzanar. He buried his feelings down deep, and we did not know how deeply he was affected until he was out of college. My brother was never able to claim an identity. He was angry at being American, for the way he was treated; he was angry at the Japanese because their actions put the whole thing in motion. He hated his Japanese appearance, yet longed to belong to the culture that he was also proud of. Low self-esteem and searching for something that would anesthetize him from his confused feelings led him to a bad crowd. He became a drug addict, opium among others. By the time we found out, he was too far gone, and he had lost his job and most of his money. We tried many times to pull him out of the dark, deep well he was drowning in, but he would not take the ropes we would throw him. It was as if he wanted to just give up. My brother fought his demons all his adult life. By the time the drug culture of the sixties became mainstream, my brother had been doing them for years. He died at the peak of the drug era, at thirty-seven years of age. I'm afraid he was a willing victim, a poster boy for that time. My parents were devastated."

"I'm sorry, Yoshito. You must think of him a lot," Rudy said, but it was more of a question.

"I do. I think about what his life would have been like if there had been no Manzanar. I think of the fun we had as boys before our world changed, and what it would have been like to have grown old together, reminiscing over more carefree memories. I think of his easy laugh, and I remember his great sensitivity. I think he must be happy now on the other side of the curtain."

"And your sister?" Rudy hoped there was a better story about her.

"Ah, my dear sister Mae. She was a delicate and beautiful flower. She had great compassion and a great love for all of us. Not surprisingly, she became a nurse. Worked all her life helping others and took care of my parents when they became old and infirmed. She was generous of spirit, and I miss her a great deal."

"What happened to her?" Rudy asked.

"She never married and lived with my parents until they died, and then continued to work in nursing. When she developed cancer over five years ago, she moved in with Grace and me and was with us the last few months of her life. Grace and she were good friends, and Grace took great care of her. We made her as comfortable as we could, and then one night while she was sleeping, she slipped to the other side to be with the rest of my family. My beloved Grace followed her three years later. So you see, Rudy, I am the last one left of my family. I think they are all waiting for me, but my time has not yet come. But one day, I will be reunited with all of them, and we will be happy together once again."

There was an awkward silence. Rudy felt so sad for his friend. How could he complain about his father not being in his life? At least he had his mother. He must remember to do something nice for her.

"In the meantime, we have this beautiful paradise which God and nature have rendered freely. We must always remember to give thanks for its beauty and for making us a part of its plan and for the friendships it has brought together."

Rudy nodded, suddenly overcome with emotion. He didn't want Yoshito to know that if he dared speak, surely his voice would crack, so he didn't say anything more. His heart expanded as he considered all that had happened this summer. He wasn't sure God existed, but he found himself giving thanks for the coolness of the shade and the warmth of the sun, for the soft gurgling of water and the rock paths that looked like rain on a river. He was suddenly aware that the colorful flowers, the fragrant roses, and full-bodied vegetables praised God too, just by being all they were created to be. He blessed the singing birds and the fluttering butterflies and the comfort of Ling who thought he was a gentle spirit. Most of all, he gave thanks for the rough and calloused hands of Jacob, Frederick, and Yoshito, that shaped and molded and toiled to care for the living things that shared this space with them. And even as he said these prayers, he understood and accepted that they had tended his heart too.

Chapter 10

Rudy's mama silently marveled at how her son had changed during the summer as he walked through the door that evening. First of all, there was no slam! Then, as he walked by, he bent down and kissed her on the cheek! What miracles were occurring that hot summer she couldn't even begin to understand, but she believed her prayers were being answered.

Rudy had changed on the outside and on the inside. Outwardly, he was taller, stood straighter, and was more muscular and tan with his usual look of distrust gone from his eyes. His body was beginning to change from a boy to a man. On the inside, her son had become more attentive, more inquisitive, asking her all kinds of questions at the dinner table. One night, Rudy asked, "What do you remember about the civil rights movement in the sixties?" Another night he asked if she knew anything about the Japanese internment camps. She gathered he was hearing things from Frederick, Jacob, and the other neighbor Yoshito. She wanted to encourage his questions but had to admit that she almost had to pull herself up off the floor a couple of times, so surprised was she at his curiosity and openness. Mealtime had gone from her trying to pry things from Rudy, to him peppering her with questions.

He was reading, too. One book only made him want to read another. He would study maps as well. She watched in amazement, praised God, and tried not to ask too many questions—she just wanted it to continue. She wondered if her son would revert to the quiet, angry, introverted boy once school began and he started spending time with those boys again. Each night when the house was quiet, she would continue her ritual of getting down on her knees and praying that God would guide her boy. Then she prayed for Jacob, Frederick, and Yoshito, too. Those men were just angels; there was no other explanation. What else could explain her son's transformation? *Lord, bless your angels that live in the three houses around the corner . . .*

Chapter 11

The summer was two thirds of the way gone. It was mid-August, and it had been a hot summer. Rudy was finally feeling at home with these three men; he felt like he was almost one of them, one of their inner circle, a member of their family—like he belonged there. Still, there was always a remoteness or cautiousness from Jacob. Rudy wanted more than anything to break down the barrier that existed between them. They'd gotten off to a rocky start, but he wanted Jacob to know that he had changed. He wanted Jacob—yes, the old Jew man—to be his friend. He cringed recalling how he used to think of Jacob.

The day that things changed was another hot day, but considerably cooler in Jacob's back yard. Still, pulling out that metal fence in the heat was hard and dirty work, but he'd found a rhythm to the digging and pulling, and it was coming easier now. Jacob would help dig now and again but mostly left Rudy to his own devises to pull out the fence after that initial blow-up they had had early on. Rudy felt comfortable now stopping occasionally for refreshment, seeking respite in the shadows and shade of trees.

It was about three o'clock in the afternoon, when Jacob called him over for some iced tea.

"We must keep ourselves hydrated in this heat. Come, come and rest; you are getting close to the end, but those last few feet of fence won't go anywhere while you sit for a minute," Jacob bid and Rudy obeyed, glad to rest and wipe away the sweat that poured profusely off his brow. He watched Jacob pour the amber liquid, heard the ice cubes clink as they hit the glass, and thought it was a beautiful sound when you were thirsty.

"I sure have enjoyed working with you this summer, Jacob. I didn't think I would, but I have. I've learned a lot, and I have enjoyed getting to know Frederick and Yoshito—and you. Now it's almost at an end." Rudy trailed off. Jacob looked at him with a startled expression. He smiled.

"When you first arrived, I didn't think you could put two words together. Thought you had quite a chip on your shoulder. I knew you didn't want to be here with us old men, eh? But you fooled me. You have been a hard worker and a good boy. Yes, you fooled an old fool. Frederick said I should give you a chance; he saw something in you."

Rudy smiled. "I'm glad he convinced you. Truthfully, Jacob, I don't know that I would have given me a chance either. But, I was a different kid then." He looked at Jacob, hoping he recognized it, looking for affirmation.

When he didn't see it, Rudy's voice became more serious. "Hey, Jacob, do you believe me? I want you to trust me now."

Jacob stopped. "What does my young Goliath mean, do I believe you?"

Rudy shook his head. "Sometimes I feel you are far away, or that when you do look at me, you don't quite know what to think of me. I guess I want you to see that I've changed. I want your approval." Jacob was surprised by this.

"You don't need my approval, Rudy. I am just an old man who sits in a garden, waiting for time to pass."

"I want it though. It's been the toughest to earn. I guess your approval would make me feel like we had turned a corner; like we both had changed from the beginning of the summer. I know I wasn't very nice when I started working here. I'm sorry about blowing up at you that time. I was just mad."

Jacob thought on this. Perhaps it was time to open up and trust this young boy, and share a bit of his story with Rudy. It's true; he did seem like a different boy.

After a long pause, Jacob replied, "I will tell you something, Rudy, that I never thought I would tell anyone. That makes you special. When I used to see and hear you around the streets with those friends of yours, saw the way you looked at me and called me Jew man, among other things . . ."

Rudy committed to himself in that moment that those boys were not his friends anymore. Never did he want to be identified with them again. Embarrassed, Rudy began, "Jacob, I'm . . . I'm so sorry. I was so stupid . . ."

Jacob put up his hand and stopped him, and leaning in, said quietly, as if telling a secret, "I used to see in you the German soldiers that terrorized my family when I was a boy. I was afraid of you, you and those boys. Can you imagine an old man like me, scared of some kids on bikes?" Jacob's voice quivered as he waved Rudy away. Embarrassed, he started to cry. Rudy was ashamed that his actions could have frightened this old, harmless man to the point of tears. Rudy wanted to comfort Jacob but didn't know how.

"Jacob, I am so sorry. I didn't mean it—I was . . ." Rudy struggled for the word Frederick had used to describe the men that killed his father. "Ignorant! I just wanted to fit in." But he knew now that those boys were cruel, and he had been too when he was with them, to Jacob, the boy in the park, the store owner, and others. He went over and knelt down on the ground next to Jacob's chair and put his arm around his back.

"What a silly old man I am, crying over a few mean boys. You must forgive me."

"It's okay, Jacob, really. I would never hurt you; you've got to believe that. Forgive me, Jacob. I'm so sorry." Rudy was now close to tears, his voice trembling. He had never asked for forgiveness from anyone.

Jacob looked up, and for the first time, really looked into Rudy's eyes and saw that they did not contain the hardness of the soldiers of war. They were young and frightened, and he saw sorrow, too. Jacob patted Rudy on the cheek and said, "Yes, I believe you, Rudy, and I trust you too, my young friend. I think you are a good boy."

And then Jacob allowed himself something that he hadn't in years: to be hugged and to hug back. He had forgotten how wonderful it felt to be embraced. How long had it been since someone had hugged him and he had returned it?

After a few minutes gathering themselves, Jacob cleared his throat and stood up, but Rudy bravely asked, "What did the German solders do to you and your family? Can you talk about it?"

Jacob walked over to the fence that had mostly fallen over, yet a few yards still remained. He touched it as it hung limply into Frederick's yard. The fence was almost down. Perhaps it was time to speak of that awful period in his life, expel some demons. He took in a deep breath and turned to look into the face of a boy who was not a German soldier. It was the face of Rudy, a boy he had come to care about a great deal despite himself; and it was Rudy who looked back. Jacob came back to the table, sat down, and said a prayer to *her* for the words and the strength to tell his story.

Chapter 12

"I was almost ten the year the Nazi party came into power. It was 1933. Seems like a long time ago to a boy of your age, but not so long ago to me. Sometimes it seems like the images are so far away, and other times when I wake up, it takes me a minute to realize I am not back there. That time was the beginning of much pain and tragedy for my family and for our Jewish community."

Jacob leaned forward, his elbows resting on his knees, and looked at the ground. After a few seconds of mentally sorting out his narrative, he continued. "My mind is racing forward, but I am getting ahead of myself. First, let me tell you about my earlier years, my family."

Jacob looked off as if into a far, distant land on the other side of a great ocean that he struggled to see.

"I grew up in Germany. Ask your teacher to show you where that is if you don't know." He looked again at Rudy and continued.

"When I was a little boy, times were happy. I had a normal childhood with friends and toys and singing and laughter. We lived in a house in Berlin near the university where my father was a college professor and taught philosophy. He made a good living, and we had a comfortable home with nice things. My mother, oh,

Rudy . . . she was a beautiful woman. She stayed at home with us children; it wasn't like today where working women are a normal thing. You know, for years I had a shawl of hers that carried the scent of her perfume. After the smell faded, I gave the shawl to Grace, Yoshito's wife. It looked better on her than wrapped in tissue paper in a drawer. Besides, my mother would have liked Grace to have it rather than me hanging on to it as if it could bring her back." Jacob paused for a moment before continuing.

"So, we lived in Berlin, a bustling city with lots of things to do and places to see. There were many cultural events and parties which my parents enjoyed and attended with their many friends, most of whom were either from the university or the neighborhood. Many of our neighborhood friends owned local businesses nearby, many of them Jewish businesses. As a young child, I knew I was Jewish, but I don't think I understood that others were not. Everyone got along; there was no derision around us being Jewish."

Here Jacob paused. His thoughts darted in and out of those secret, dark places that he had kept locked for so many years. It was time to talk about *her*, and he wondered if he had the courage to say her name out loud after all these years.

Rudy looked at him, wondering, but not saying anything, sensing that Jacob was reaching back for something, something difficult for him to grasp. A great sigh burdened down with vast sadness escaped from the depth of his gut. With the faintest of breezes blowing past, he looked Rudy directly in the eyes with the most anguished, yet tender, expression Rudy had ever seen and resumed in a voice that was quiet and reverent, as if he were talking in church.

"I had a sister, my twin, and her name was . . . Blanca. How very beautiful she was, with a laugh that could melt the meanest and hardest of hearts and eyes that out-twinkled the brightest of stars. Do you know anyone like that?" he asked, but didn't wait for an answer.

"We were the best of friends. Yes, even at that age when brothers and sisters quarrel and squabble, and we did too mind you, but in the end, we were inseparable. Maybe it's because we were twins that we were so close; I don't know. I only know that I loved her and always wanted to protect her."

Anguish washed across Jacob's face, and Rudy wanted to ask what happened to her, but instinctively knew that in these moments of revelation, all his questions would be answered. He also understood the profound trust that Jacob was putting in him, and he knew he would not betray that trust.

Another breeze blew by Jacob's face, and it was so gentle, so reassuring, he wondered if it was *her*. Gaining his composure, Jacob began again. Having said her name, having its wonderful sound roll off his tongue once again, he knew now that he could not stop.

"You know, I have not said her name since I told Frederick and Yoshito decades ago—thought I could not say her name again without dying. It doesn't hurt as bad as I thought it would," he said, and smiled briefly at Rudy with sad eyes.

"I do not remember much those first years after Hitler came into power, as I was still a young boy with other things on my mind, like homework and playing ball with my friends. However, things were happening; subtle at first then becoming more obvious as time went on. Old classmates after a time would no longer play with me, and there were suddenly smirks and comments from some of the kids at school who had always been mean and picked on the weaker kids but now directed their insults at me and my sister. I remember once bloodying the nose of a boy who taunted Blanca. He ran away, but yelled back to me that I would be sorry—that we were nothing but filthy Jews. At first I was merely puzzled, but as time went by and I grew up, I began to understand how things had changed."

Rudy thought briefly about those boys he used to hang out with and realized there was no difference between them and this bully.

"My parents tried very hard to hide what was happening around us—to keep us innocent for as long as they could—until we were a bit older. How do you explain what was happening to friends and family and us was because we were Jewish? To this day, looking at history and what was happening, I can't help but wonder why my parents didn't leave Germany while they still could. I suppose by the time they understood that the horrific rumors were in fact true, it was too late to get out.

"Yet, all the warnings were there. Jewish children were banned from attending school. My father ultimately lost his job. By 1936, the Nazis were boycotting Jewish-owned businesses. I think November 1938 was a turning point. There was the 'Night of Broken Glass,' or *Kristallnacht*. That night, Nazis terrorized Jews in Germany and Austria by ransacking and destroying businesses, breaking storefronts, sponsoring anti-Jewish riots, burning synagogues, and breaking into homes—ultimately arresting thirty thousand Jews and killing others. I don't know how we escaped being terrorized that night. Perhaps it was because my father was an 'educated' Jew. Who knows how their minds worked? My father was much like Frederick's and Yoshito's; he was not a coward but knew it was safer to keep a low profile and not speak out. Outraged friends of ours who had spoken publicly about the injustice disappeared at night. We know now that they were taken to Dachau, one of the concentration camps. Many were beaten to death. At the time, we just knew that people were disappearing during that night and other nights that followed. We lived in terror for years. In 1939, we were all forced to wear arm bands displaying the Star of David. We became easy targets if seen on the streets by an SS; they would find any reason to beat or kill us. We only survived because of the generosity of some of our Christian friends, but it was dangerous for anyone to help us. The Kleins would sneak us baked bread in laundry; the Reinholms, next door, would wrap fruit and vegetables in a burlap bag and bury it in a hole under our shared fence at night. Then we would dig a hole on our side while it was still dark and pull out the bag. We would have starved if not for these friends. It was a very dangerous business, and they took a huge risk helping us. Rudy, I have not forgotten them one day of my life, and I pray for them every time I drop to my knees.

"Then, one night it happened to us. It was 1940. There was a pounding on the door at two in the morning. That's the way they did it, you know; anything that would make you more frightened, break down your defenses. What came next felt like the beginning of the end. It is the time when all the color went out of my life and the world turned into shades of gray."

Jacob paused, not knowing if he could go on. Yet there was a voice in his head—*her* voice—guiding him, encouraging him to tell it all, to finally spit the bile and venom out of his mouth that he might begin to heal.

Rudy looked at Jacob with sad eyes, feeling the pain with him. He reached out and took Jacob's hand, yet didn't say a word.

Appearing unaware of Rudy's hand on his, Jacob continued, almost as fearful as if reliving it in that moment, back in that house and not sitting with Rudy under the leafy green shade of a tree in his garden.

"My father rushed out of bed to the door, and by then we were hearing yelling. They were shouting at my father to round up his family. When my father didn't move fast enough, they pushed him aside to the ground and went through the house to each of our rooms to gather us together. They had their guns out, and when we were together, we were told we had ten minutes to change into warm traveling clothes and that we could bring one suitcase each of clothing. One of the soldiers was staring at my sister, looking her up and down in a disgusting manner. He was making rude comments to one of the others about my sister's beauty and how unfortunate that she was a Jew. Blanca and I were by then a little older than you, nearly seventeen, and she was beautiful, too beautiful. Shortly after we had each gone to our rooms to pack, the one soldier entered my sister's room and closed the door. Suddenly, I heard Blanca screaming and the Nazi soldier laughing. Then I heard a hard slap, and for a moment there was silence. Then Blanca continued her screaming. I tried to get into the room, but the other soldiers prevented me, and one of them finally hit me with the handle of his gun."

For a moment, Rudy saw the kid in the park being punched and hitting the ground while he stood and watched. Jacob's voice brought him back to in the moment.

"As I teetered back and began to lose consciousness, I heard my sister's fading screaming turn to crying. I heard my mother wailing, as if she were at the end of the tunnel. I felt my father at my side, and then I blacked out for a short time.

"When I awakened, everyone was in the front hallway, including myself. My sister was dressed and in a coat, her face swollen and beginning to color from being struck and from crying. My mother had her arm around her helping her navigate, as she appeared to be in a daze. Someone had put boots on my feet, and my father was lifting me up, pulling my arm around his neck so that he could help me walk until I regained full consciousness. They were not going to wait, you see. I either moved or would be shot. I wanted to go to my sister, but I was still a bit dizzy, just trying to put one foot in front of the other, moving as if I had had too much to drink. As my mother tried to put my arms through my coat as my father held me up, we were herded into a truck where others that we knew and some that we didn't were seated. All had frightened looks on their face; no one was speaking. They reached out and helped us up onto the truck. No one asked questions about me or Blanca. They could piece it together. You see, everyone knew she had been raped. That ugly, vile-mouthed monster had violated my beautiful, innocent, darling sister." And with this Jacob put his head down into his arms and sobbed like he had not sobbed since being liberated.

Minutes passed. Rudy sat next to Jacob and just let him cry. Tears ran down Rudy's face silently at the sight, and reaching out, he put his arm around Jacob's back. His heart was bursting with love for this man, with such compassion for all he had endured and held in all these years. He understood Jacob's reticence toward him and felt guilty for being the reminder, the trigger of his past.

After a while, Jacob looked up, wiping his eyes. Rudy asked, "You okay, Jacob? Is there anything I can get you?"

Jacob just shook his head and patted his cheek. "Forgive an old man crying like a baby. Just stay here and let me finish what I have begun."

"Okay, Jacob, okay." Jacob blew his nose on an old handkerchief and took a deep breath. After a minute, he continued on.

"My mother sat on one side of Blanca and I sat on the other. I reached out to take her hand, but there was no reaction; she just stared, not at me, not at anything, just a blank, empty stare. My father watched with an anguished look on his face. I knew he wanted to kill the man who had done this to his beloved daughter, but all that would accomplish was being killed himself. And then who would be there to look after us? My father, Rudy, was a good man. He kept his anger bottled up just so he could stay with his family. He didn't yet know there was nothing he could do to protect us.

"The truck took us to the train station where a long line of railway cars with their side doors gaping open wide waited to transport us to places unknown. We didn't know where we were going; we only knew it couldn't be good. We knew that people who disappeared in the middle of the night were not seen again. The boxcars were empty but for hay strewn on the floor. There were no beds, no chairs, no heat, no toilets, only a bucket in the middle of each car. No privacy either. We were packed so tightly, like sardines in a can; most of us had to stand the entire journey, let the old folks and the sick sit or lie down if possible. The car began to stink as the bucket filled. We had small air vents which circulated frigid air. We prayed to get to our destination, for surely it would be better than these conditions. How little we knew—how innocent we were of what was coming. We were on the train for days and realized that we had left Germany behind and moved into western Poland. Some people speculated about where we were headed, others had heard things, terrible things, but surely these stories could not be true.

"Blanca was quiet during the trip and ate very little of what we had brought with us hidden in our clothes. The rhythm of the moving train seemed to keep her lulled in a near catatonic state—the twinkle gone from her eyes. Every now and then, tears would flow from them, yet there were no sobs, no sounds, as if the act of crying were not connected to any thought process. As hard as I tried, she could draw no comfort from me. How bitter I felt. I had failed to protect the sister I loved as dear as myself. Little did I know that time in the train would be the last I would be with her.

"We finally arrived at our destination. It was raining and cold when we got there. We had arrived at Auschwitz."

Rudy looked shocked. He had heard stories of what happened there—stories too hard to believe.

"Ah, I see by the look on your face that you have heard of Auschwitz."

Rudy nodded,. "I never heard of anyone surviving."

"Many times I have wondered if it would have been better for me if I had not survived. My entire family died there, Rudy. Why was I spared? Spared to remember the brutality, the inhumanity, and the terror? Spared to remember my family, all gone too soon in horrible deaths? It has not been an easy life. I have not been able to move past it, the way Yoshito and Frederick have moved beyond their painful histories. It still haunts me, even in my dreams, as if it were yesterday." Jacob struggled to regain his composure.

"Maybe today, Rudy, you are helping me. I told you, I have not shared this story with anyone for decades. But in telling you, I am somehow beginning to feel less burdened, less fearful. I am afraid that in my giving, you, my friend, may now carry some of it with you for the rest of your life. Forgive me for that." Jacob patted him on the back, and Rudy nodded his understanding.

"Tell me the rest, Jacob. I can take it. How did you survive? What happened there?" Rudy questioned, and Jacob slipped back into that time and place.

"Bad things happened almost immediately. When they opened the car door, it was very cold and wet. It had been raining and now a light, persistent drizzle fell. Most surely it was heaven weeping. We could see that the women and men were being divided; women going one way, men going another. My family panicked. My father quickly told us that if we were separated, we should find our way back to the Reinholms' after the war. They would take care of us until we could all get there. Father, mother, and I agreed. My sister, with the terror of a caged animal and a wildness in her eyes, said to me in a voice that was too calm, too determined, 'I can't do this, Jacob. I can't bear anymore. I'm afraid, Jacob! I am too afraid.' Then she added, 'Remember I love you and explain to mommy and father.' As I held her hand, I tried to assure her that she just needed to do as she was told; be strong and we would all be together again someday, and what had happened would be in the past. She just looked at me blankly as we were pushed along with the other people. Soon our hands were separated by the throng of others being pushed along. I kept yelling not to give up. My father and I managed to push my mother through those ahead of us to ensure she stayed with Blanca. My father and I were veered off into another direction. We waved and yelled I love you along with the other husbands and fathers being separated from their families. My mother's only thought was to stay close to Blanca, and she did not look back.

"We did not see them again, and little did I know that my sister would die within hours. We heard later that after we were separated, the fit women were taken to an area where they were stripped of their belongings, including their clothes and their shoes. They were then led to an area where their heads were shaved. It would be humiliating for anyone, but my sister . . . well, she was in a fragile state of mind. They were issued gray-colored dresses and wood shoes, and then marched to their barracks. On the way, they were forced to walk by a huge pit. Inside there were dead, naked bodies, along with the barely living bodies of the too old and infirmed who were of no good to the work camp. They were left to die along with the dead in the freezing cold. Through the camp grapevine, my father and I found out that my sister, upon seeing the bodies in the pit, began screaming hysterically. My mother tried to quiet her, but my sister had lost her mind. An SS soldier came up to them, threatening them, ordering my sister to stop. My mother pleaded with her, but Blanca was inconsolable and kept screaming. The soldier dragged her out of line, pushed her in the pit, and shot her. Her screaming stopped, and she was gone from this world—just like that.

"Then without so much as an afterthought, as if he had just kicked some trash out of his path, the soldier ordered the others to move on. The surrounding women grabbed my screaming and crying mother, quieting her and telling her to move on or she would be joining her daughter. I'm sure the only reason my mother did not jump in after Blanca was the thought of my father and me.

"I can only imagine my mother's heartbreak; I saw the look of grief seize my father's face when we were told the story, saw the pain in his eyes. I think he aged ten years in that moment. I know my heart broke; my beloved sister, my twin—a part of me was dead. I think we were both numb, almost confused by what we were hearing, that we were not able to even cry. Maybe it had been a mistake, maybe it was another young girl named Blanca. But we knew better, knew the tenuous, delicate state my sister had been in. The men around us tried to console us and offered up prayers for the dead. I don't know what I would have done had I been there when it happened; probably would have got myself shot, too. Rudy, I hate the monster that did that to my sister. I hate the pain my mother suffered watching her daughter being handled like she was less than nothing, but a part of me is so grateful that she did not have to endure the years and untold horrors in that camp. She was with God at last where she belonged—and there were many times I wished I were with her."

"Don't say that, Jacob," Rudy begged.

In a voice charged with anger, Jacob replied, "Rudy, you think we live in a hard world, but you are still very innocent. Terrible, unspeakable acts happened while I was there: live babies thrown into bonfires, old people beaten, medical experiments conducted on us like we were guinea pigs, and yes, the gas chambers and the crematoriums. What kind of human beings can do those things? I still don't understand it after decades of living with those memories."

After a time, Jacob cleared his throat, and in a quieter voice said, "I suppose I never will. Only God can understand the complexities of each human heart and will judge accordingly."

"Do you still believe in God, I mean, after all that you went through?" Rudy asked tentatively.

"That's a big question for a young man. But the answer is easy: with all my heart, Rudy. I'm afraid He may be disappointed in me, however. I stopped going to temple when I could not rid myself of the nightmares, even though I knew it was not God that did this to us. It was human beings who made a pact with the devil. I know that God wept with us in our bondage and marched with the Allies and rejoiced when we were liberated. It was God that helped me live on when I didn't know if I wanted to, who steered me to this house, next door to two men who would understand me and help me and fill my loneliness; it was God that whispered your name into Frederick's ear and who sent you to pull down this fence. Oh, yes, Rudy, I believe in God." Jacob studied Rudy's face trying to read his thoughts.

"Sometimes in searching for answers to things we can't understand, we humans find it easier to blame God instead of our own free will. But you have asked a big question which you will have to answer for yourself. You're a smart boy, Rudy. Just look around, and you will feel the answer in your soul."

Rudy thought of his mother dragging him to church each Sunday. He had seen her praying a million times and thought it was nonsense, but now he wondered if maybe God really did exist, did listen to prayers. If Jacob and Frederick and Yoshito all believed after what they had been through, perhaps there was something to it. Maybe he would listen more closely the next time he went with her, listen more to what the pastor said. Jacob interrupted his thoughts.

"But let me continue. My father and I were issued striped work clothes that were not nearly warm enough, and we were housed in overcrowded barracks, hundreds of men to a barrack, several to a bunk. Everyone received a tattooed number on their arm. That's all we were, a number," he said, as he showed the now familiar inside of his forearm to Rudy.

"My father and I were lucky that we were healthy and strong. We were put to work almost immediately after getting there. We dug pits mostly, for the dead. It was a horrible job, but we knew as long as we worked hard and stayed out of trouble, we might survive and not end up in the pit or gas chamber ourselves. That is, if we could avoid the illnesses in the camps. There was so much death, so many diseases: dysentery, pneumonia, tuberculosis, typhus, and then just exhaustion from being malnourished and being worked to death. Someone might have a broken bone or a cut, but with no medical attention, the infection could kill them. You could only pray to God in heaven to die quickly if that was your fate, otherwise you would end up in the pit—alive or dead—or later on in the crematorium. The smell of death was everywhere; even outdoors it seemed to live in your uniform, stay permanently housed in your nostrils. It is something I will never forget.

"On the second morning after walking out of the camp gates forever, I was finally far enough away that when I went outside and breathed in fresh air. I finally did not smell burning flesh and rot. Do you know what I did, Rudy? I wept for joy. I cried and cried and cried. I was so happy, yet so sad. I think some of those tears were also for my family." Again, Jacob paused, trying to reign in his emotions.

"But I am moving ahead in my story. My father and I somehow survived for years without too much incident. Oh, we got very skinny, just bags of bones, but we were able to keep relatively disease-free. We saw terrible things being done to others, but somehow we were able to stay under the radar. My father suffered great depression over Blanca's death. I think he blamed himself for keeping us so innocent for so long, saying that Blanca may have coped better had she been more aware of what was happening. I tried to reassure him and refocus his thoughts on what life would be like after the war, but even that was a challenge. We had heard nothing of my mother.

"There was a lot of turmoil going on the last months before the war ended. In October 1944, SS soldiers began rounding us up telling us we were moving to another camp and that we were walking for part of the way, another train for the remainder of the trip. The sick and the children were being left behind, to die no doubt. These evacuations were called the death marches. It was extremely cold outside, and my father and I wondered if we could survive. We didn't understand what was happening then, but we know now that the German military leaders were getting scared. They wanted to leave the scene of the crime and take as much of the evidence with them—and hoped that we would die along the way. The journey was brutal; we lost half the number we started with. Men were left to die if they were weak or sick, or were shot along the way. There was little food, and the temperatures were freezing. We ate snow for water. My father made the trip, but his strength and stamina clearly deteriorated. We ended up at Bergen-Belsen, another concentration camp.

"Although there was always talk of the war ending, most of it was wishful thinking to keep us alive. But after the move from Auschwitz, the rumors seemed more believable than ever; yet, how could we get our hopes up? Right around Chanukah, my father caught pneumonia. He was very ill but still went out on work detail. Each night we said our prayers which were so dear to my father. You asked if I believe in God? At that time, secretly I wondered where God had gone. I did not yet understand the complexities of free will and to what extent Hitler had mesmerized so many German people.

"Each day, I covered for my father as much as possible, but finally the time came when he could no longer get out of bed to go to work. I pleaded with him, encouraging him with hope that the war would soon be ending and we would be reunited with my mother. He would say, 'Yes, yes, my son. We will be together soon,' but I believe he knew he would not be there for that reunion. On the last morning of his life, he patted my cheek before I left for work detail. He said, 'Jacob, my only son and now my only child, you are a good boy and will be a good man. God is good. Remember that.' All I could say was, 'Yes, papa. God is good.' I wished I had told him that I loved him, that he had been a good father, that he had kept me alive all these years; but I didn't. When I returned that night, his body was gone—to the pit, to the crematorium, I never knew. That night, I wept myself to sleep, but I resolved to live to find and take care of my mother.

"In January of 1945, we did not know it, but Soviet armies were closing in on Auschwitz. In those last days, SS soldiers were told to blow up the crematoriums—you know, get rid of the evidence. There are still some there to this day, a testament to what occurred. On April 15, 1945, British troops liberated us at last. They found sixty thousand survivors and twenty-seven thousand unburied corpses piled in heaps. I found out in the days that followed that my mother had died of tuberculosis within one year of coming into the camp. How could that be, I asked myself? I had only stayed alive to take care of her once my father had died. Now, I was left on my own. The grief, anger, and hopelessness were almost unbearable.

Now, I had only one goal: to go home and get to the Reinholms' as my father had instructed. Maybe it was a mistake, and Momma would be there waiting for me, to hug me and comfort me the way she did when I was a small boy. With every last ounce of strength and determination in my body, I made my way back to Berlin, even though I had heard so much of the city was destroyed. Some buildings were barely standing, others unscathed. Very few people had stayed in Berlin, yet some had nowhere else to go. Still, I was determined. I hitched rides with army trucks. I walked and I accepted help and warmer clothes from strangers. I must have looked like a half dead skeleton when I knocked on the Reinholms' door. I was so thin that my bones protruded everywhere; my head was shaved and I had open sores on my body. Mrs. Reinholm answered the door and didn't recognize me at first; she thought I was a scavenger. When I addressed her and asked if my mother had made it back, she looked at me hard, and then said, "Oh, my God, Jacob, what have they done to you? She took me in her arms and led me into the house screaming for her husband. They immediately gave me food and drink and then sent me upstairs for a hot bath—the first I had taken in almost five years. Then I slept for two days."

"Your mother never came, did she?" Rudy asked, knowing the answer. Jacob shook his head.

"While building back up my strength and putting some meat on these bones, I waited for her, looking out the window, jumping every time someone came to the door. Of course, my mother was dead. I came to accept that with the help of the Reinholms. They were very good to me. They let me stay with them for as long as I wanted. Our home had been next door, but there was nothing left. In those years we were gone, everything had been ransacked. The Reinholms did manage to sneak in the night we were taken and get some of our belongings out before the authorities and pillagers came through. I was grateful to have something that my parents and Blanca had touched: my mother's shawl, a picture they had admired, a clock from the hallway, the brush and mirror from Blanca's room, some old photos, my father's embroidered handkerchiefs. I walked through the house once, but it no longer felt like home. There were dark and unexpected shadows in places I seemed to remember as being bright and gay. I was only in there for a few minutes before I was burdened with such sadness. Berlin itself was not the city I had left, so much of it destroyed and bombed.

"In the months following the end of the war, as Berlin began to rebuild, I got a clerical job in one of the businesses where the owners had known and liked my parents, and I tried to figure out what I wanted to do. I think they felt sorry for me. But I was grateful and accepted their pity. I think they may have also felt a little guilty as well. What had been done to me was the least of what their great führer had done. I somehow had survived that madman's lunacy. But I did not want them to regret their kindness toward me. I worked hard, was good with numbers, and made myself useful. I think in the end, they were sorry to see me leave.

"I had been with the Reinholms just under two years on the day that I told them I had bought a ticket to America. Mr. and Mrs. Reinholm cried; they thought of me as a son. They then brought out an envelope and handed it to me. Years before our evacuation, after it was too late for our escape out of Germany, my father gave the Reinholms the equivalent of two hundred dollars—a lot of money for that time. He asked them to hold it, in case any of us survived the war. If none of us came back, it was theirs for helping us. Without any thought of their own gain, they gave it to me, telling me they had known this day would come and that I would need the money to start a new life. How we hugged that day. They wished me well and told me to keep in touch. I promised I would.

"As good as the Reinholms had been to me, there was nothing to keep me in Germany any longer, and how could I stay and not be haunted by memories of what had been? My family was all dead. I needed to move far away.

"My mother had a cousin who lived in Los Angeles, and I had written to him asking if I could stay with him until I got settled. He was more than generous and happy to hear that someone from his extended family had survived the war. It was a long journey, but every mile that passed by my window on the ship, the train, and the bus seemed to distance me from the camp and from the country I could not call home any longer.

"I came to America and spent another year with my cousin. I got a job and went to school, saved some money. America was very good to me; she adopted a poor, beaten-down immigrant, and made him her own. Don't ever underestimate what you can do in this country, Rudy . . . what you can be if you work hard. I'm not saying it will be easy. What would be the point if everything was just handed to you? You see the circumstances I came from and how I was able to create a future, buy this house. You know, at one time, this was considered a good neighborhood. Now I want you to succeed, be anything you want to be, but don't expect it to drop in your lap. But I do promise you that everything you can dream of is out there waiting for you, if you try. Promise me you will try, that you will try very hard, Rudy."

Rudy thought about it. He was not used to thinking about working hard as a good thing or that obstacles served a purpose. But he found himself nodding and saying that yes, he would try. He would not give up. If Jacob could do it, so could he—and he found he actually believed it.

"So, now you know it all, Rudy," he said as he let out a big sigh of relief. "I am glad I told you. Blanca helped me today—yes, I think that must be so." Rudy just nodded.

"Were you ever married, Jacob?"

"Ah no, unfortunately I was not lucky in the romance department. It was my own fault. I was always afraid to get too close to people. Afraid I would lose them and not be able to endure it. So I pushed everyone away. I see this all clearly now that I am an old man. You will find many decades from now that your eyesight will fade as you get old, but your inner eyesight will see things more clearly than when you are young. You gain a wisdom that in earlier years you cannot possess because you have not experienced enough, seen enough. When you are old like me, that is when you finally understand your own heart and soul. Yet, I see that even now I am still learning. You see, I was afraid of you and your friends, Rudy—you made me confront the past. And I find that finally standing up to it with you next to me has made me feel freer and lighter and . . . I think happier than I have in years! I feel as if a great burden has been lifted off my chest, a fear gone from my heart; fear that has been replaced with hope. So you see? There is still much for me to learn even as an old man."

"You're not afraid of me anymore, are you Jacob?"

"No, my fearless friend; in fact, I thank you." With great emotion, he continued. "I know now that I can talk about Blanca without my heart breaking. I think you did that for me."

Rudy returned Jacob's smile. Rudy felt elated. He had done this for Jacob—a poor, know-nothing, fatherless kid in the bad part of town. This is what it felt like to give. As long as he lived, Rudy never wanted to forget these moments with Jacob.

Jacob took a deep breath in his lovely garden. The air smelled fresh and clean and fragrant. As he looked around, the colors popped. How much he loved this place.

Near the back of the property, the remaining feet of fence hung to one side, barely holding on. "Ah, I hear the birds again. It must be close to dinner time. Let's call it a day, Rudy. I'm afraid I am all worn out. I think I may sleep well tonight. You're a good boy. Now go on home to your mother and tomorrow . . . well, tomorrow, we will finally tear down the rest of that damn fence."

Chapter 13

The next day, Rudy and Jacob worked on pulling down the last few feet of the fence. Frederick and Yoshito both came to help where they could. It was the end of a great battle, and the war was over.

Jacob seemed like a young man again. He seemed more vibrant, more alive, rejuvenated.

"How'd you sleep, Jacob?" Rudy asked.

"Like a baby in the arms of an angel," he replied with a wink and a smile. Frederick and Yoshito noticed the change in Jacob too.

"Jacob, if you were a younger man, I'd say you were in love!" Frederick laughed.

"Don't be silly, Frederick. What? Can't a man be happy? Can't a man take pleasure being in his yard with nature and God all around, working side by side with his best friends?"

Yoshito saw the smile on Rudy's face and responded, "Of course, Jacob. We are happy to be here to see the final stages of the fence coming down; we have all waited for this occasion. We have a great feast planned to celebrate this evening. Rudy, we thought you should invite your mother. Would she like to join us for dinner here in the yard? You can show her how hard you worked this summer."

Rudy looked at the others. "Well, yeah, I'd like that. Is it okay with all of you?"

"Of course!" Frederick replied enthusiastically.

"And you Jacob, it is okay with you?" Rudy asked.

"Rudy, it's about time I met the woman that has done such a fine job raising you. And she probably would like to meet me and Yoshito; see if we measure up to Frederick. She probably would like to see who you have been spending your time with all summer."

Rudy smiled broadly. "Okay, great, I'll let her know. Do you mind if I use your phone to call her at work?"

"No, go ahead. Just watch those dirty hands of yours. Wash them in the sink before you use the phone. It's in the living room. Go on."

Rudy ran to the back door and entered. He was smiling. His mother knew Frederick from church, but he wanted his mother to meet the others and really get to know them as he had.

He had only been in Jacob's home to use the bathroom. He hadn't seen the rest of it, only the little bit he had seen through the door his first day. How that seemed like a lifetime ago—actually three lifetimes, Frederick's, Yoshito's, and Jacob's. One day he would have a story to tell, and he knew this would be an important chapter in his tale.

Rudy dialed his mother's number at work. "Mama? It's Rudy. No, nothing is wrong. Really. Mama, listen . . . can you come over to Jacob's tonight and have dinner with all the guys? Yes, mama, of course, I'll be there too. It's kind of a celebration for taking down the fence. I'd really like you to meet them. Great. Can you come from work? Okay, sure, go ahead and change clothes first, but then come right over! Okay. Bye. Mama? I love you."

Rudy's mother sat at the other end with the phone still up to her ear and tears in her eyes long after Rudy had disconnected. Her son had not said I love you since he was a small child. Yes, she absolutely, positively wanted to have dinner with these men. They must be quite extraordinary, and she wouldn't miss this opportunity for anything.

Chapter 14

Rudy kept watching out for his mother by running from back yard to front yard every few minutes. Finally, he saw her turn the corner. Running to the back yard like an excited school child, he yelled to the others, "She's coming!"

"I would not recognize that boy as the same one who came to my door just over two months ago," Jacob mused.

"I think our young friend has changed, but I think we have too," Yoshito offered.

"Truer words were never spoken, my friend. You know, I told him about Blanca and my parents. That is the change you noticed, Frederick. Somehow telling him changed me. I think I have finally banished those fears that have haunted me."

"Just like you tore down that fence," Yoshito offered nodding to the others, just before they turned to see Rudy's mother walking up Jacob's driveway with Rudy by her side.

For just a moment as she turned the corner into the yard, she stopped, her eyes wide and her mouth agape. She looked around her.

"This is like being in heaven. I had no idea this existed behind your homes. Rudy, you said it was beautiful, but never in my wildest imagination . . ."

"Words don't do it justice, do they?" he said proudly as if somehow he were a part of its creation. Jacob, Frederick, and Yoshito smiled modestly.

"No, you are absolutely right about that. And these gentlemen are the masterminds behind this beauty? Hello, Frederick," she said as she approached the men and put out her hand to shake Frederick's. She wanted to hug each of her angels, but thought she should restrain herself at least through the introductions.

"Hello, Julia. How are you?" he asked, and took her hand in both of his. Standing next to him was a shorter, thin, older Asian man, and next to him another older gent who was stockier but surprisingly muscled.

"Julia, allow me to introduce you to Jacob and Yoshito. Yoshito here owns the house on the other side of mine, and this is Jacob's home."

"It's wonderful meeting you all. Thank you for letting Rudy work here this summer. Your yards are just amazing!"

"Thank you, Julia. Rudy helped us pull down the stubborn fence that separated my yard from the others. Now, with your son's help, that fence is down. He's a fine boy; you should be very proud," Jacob praised, patting Rudy on the back and giving him a smile.

"Mama, let me show you around. Is it all right, guys?"

"Of course, Rudy, go and show her the results of your hard work," Jacob offered.

Julia followed Rudy, her smile permanently set on her face. Rudy directed her through the winding twists and turns of the garden paths to start out his tour at Yoshito's. Here he showed her the mosaic stone path that resembled a river flowing toward the water basin, the *Tsukubai*, and told her how one must assume a position of humility to use it. Leading her farther back into the garden past the *ishi toro*, he lovingly pointed out Yoshito's place of meditation and prayer with such reverence that Julia thought she would cry. When Rudy picked up Yoshito's cat Ling and kissed it and rubbed his face into Ling's cheek, Julia's breath was taken away by the display of tenderness. He then led her to the spot that changed Frederick's life and was the beginning of the entire garden, the place where singing voices were heard and where the compass stood atop the pedestal to designate the spot. Rudy encouraged Julia to close her eyes and listen for the voices. When she said she didn't hear anything, Rudy assured her she would one day, as Frederick had assured him and that he now believed. Finally, he showed her where the fence had been, and told her how bringing down that fence with Jacob had been one of the most important things he had ever done. Julia could only listen disbelievingly. Was this the same boy she had fought with at the beginning of summer over this job? *Thank you, Jesus, for listening to a mother's prayer!* was all she could repeat to herself over and over.

The men busied themselves preparing the dinner table and setting the food on the table. Rudy came back and helped while his mother watched in amazement.

"Wait, don't forget the nectar of the gods!" Rudy yelled to Frederick as he brought out the last of the serving dishes.

"The what?" Julia asked.

"It's Frederick's iced tea. We call it the nectar of the gods," and they all laughed. And when at last drinks were in hand, Frederick toasted Rudy and Jacob for finishing the job, and Jacob let out a resounding "*L'chaim,*" and meant it for the first time in a very long time.

That evening they sat, laughed, talked, and ate dishes prepared by each of the men: Frederick made southern fried chicken; Yoshito prepared tempura with vegetables from the garden, along with a cabbage, noodle, and peanut salad; Jacob made rolls and cooked corn on the cob. Julia promised to bake a pie and bring it by one evening. Most of all, Julia watched her son in full bloom. He joked and laughed easily with these men, patted them on the back, smiled smiles that normally would have been reserved for a beloved father or grandfather. These men had worked a miracle with her boy, and watching, she couldn't guess how it had happened, only that it had.

As the evening moved into twilight, candles and lamps were lit and good-byes said with promises of more of these dinners and Julia's pie. Julia hugged each man and thanked them for what they had given to her boy.

As Rudy and his mother were walking down the driveway, Rudy ran back. "Do you think it would be okay if I told your stories to my mother?" Rudy asked tentatively. "I want her to know you the way I do."

Jacob looked around to the others who nodded to him. Then Jacob turned to Rudy and said, "Yes, yes, I think that would be fine with us. But you must remember to handle these memories with care and know that they are real." Jacob patted Rudy's cheek, and Rudy nodded his understanding.

Watching him run to meet up with his mother who was waiting for him, Jacob said to the others, "He's a good boy. He deserves a better start to life." The others could only nod in agreement.

"Frederick? Yoshito? I have a proposition for you. Have a seat." And so the three men sat back down again and talked into the night, their words and intentions floating off and dissolving into the night sky.

Chapter 15

The next day, Rudy arrived at Jacob's early in the morning as he had done all summer long.

"What brings my warrior friend out of bed this early? The fence is down; you have earned some well-deserved rest," Jacob said.

"Just thought I would come and help you clean up." Jacob nodded his approval.

"Truth is, I'm going to miss coming over every day, working in the garden with you," Rudy admitted.

Jacob smiled. "Truth is, I am going to miss you too when you go back to school."

"Ugh, school," Rudy said sadly.

"What's wrong? School is a great thing," Jacob replied.

"I know. You know those guys that I was hanging out with at the end of the school year? Well, I've kind of blown them off this summer. I'm not sure how they will react. Truth is, I don't want them as friends anymore. So I don't really have any friends at school now."

"I see," Jacob replied, nodding understanding.

"I learned so much from you and the other guys this summer. To tell you the truth, I was never too good at schoolwork, but I want to do better now; I want to make something of myself. I guess

I'm just nervous about what the kids will say. I'm afraid that I've changed and they haven't, or that they've changed in other ways."

"Yes, that is quite a dilemma. But, I have a feeling things will work out. They always do. Come; help an old man fill the gap where we pulled out the last of that stubborn fence."

Together Rudy and Jacob planted some new plants and added soil to fill the trench where the fence had been dug out. Rudy relished the warmth and feel of manure and peat moss in his hands mixed with the soil, and he wished these summer days could go on forever. How he dreaded the prospect of going back to school with the old gang waiting for him—to tease and taunt him. He wondered if his fate was to be the next boy on the ground having been beat up. Well, he just had to put it out of his mind for today and enjoy the last couple of weeks before school started.

The day had a relaxed feel. The pressure of bringing down the fence was gone. Now they could work, rest, work again, visit with Frederick and Yoshito, and go examine and help out with their projects. Later that day, when the four of them were gathered together, Jacob casually asked if his mother and he would like to come for another picnic dinner Saturday evening. Rudy excitedly said he was 99 percent sure they could make it.

"Talk to your mother about it tonight, and let us know tomorrow. That will give us a day to create our feast. Summer is coming to an end," Jacob replied.

That night at home, Julia was swept up in Rudy's enthusiasm and agreed to attend, deciding to bring over the pie she had promised. She had heard the stories of these remarkable men and wanted Rudy to spend as much time with them as possible. These were men that would be her son's role models, help him navigate through the difficulties of growing up in a way she couldn't.

As Rudy lay in bed that night, and for the first time ever, he closed his eyes and said a prayer, thanking whoever was listening, for the three old men with calloused hands.

Chapter 16

It seemed that everyone stopped talking at about the same time. Stomachs were full, compliments on the pie delivered, laughter eased, conversation wound down. The changing light seemed to signal the time to begin clearing dishes and getting ready to go home.

Frederick and Yoshito looked at Jacob, and he nodded understanding.

"Rudy, Julia, the three of us would like to discuss something with you."

Jacob had their attention.

"Rudy, you and I discussed your uneasiness about returning to the school with that old group of kids waiting for you."

Julia looked at Rudy, surprised that he had the same worries she had, that he had given up this gang of boys.

"So, the three of us have a proposition for you. How would you feel about switching schools?"

Rudy was stunned. "What do you mean? Where would I go? It's the only school in the district." Julia looked bewildered too.

"It's the only public school. What about a private school?"

"We can't afford that Jacob," Julia stated, not understanding his meaning.

"No, but the three of us can afford it."

Rudy and Julia looked at them and then at each other.

"That's very kind, but we couldn't allow you to do that," Julia protested, with Rudy nodding his agreement, yet giving his mother a questioning look.

"Yeah, you guys can't do that."

"Oh no, Mister Naysayer? Why not? Look, we want to do this. We have come to care a great deal for you, Rudy. I used to think you were Mister Chip-on-Your-Shoulder, but Frederick saw something in you first, and now we all see it. A fire, a great potential to be anything you want to be. We don't want you to lose that. We want you to have a great education. Now, that means you will have to buckle down and do real studying every night after school. No more messing around."

Rudy nodded as if already agreeing. Julia looked at them, wondering if she could agree to accept this generosity.

Jacob leaned over and put his hand across Rudy's arm and spoke to him as if no one else were around—like a father would to a son, or in this case a grandfather to a beloved grandson.

"Look, Rudy, I don't want you to hang around with those boys, those boys who are headed down the wrong road. Where they are going is not a place we want you to be. I know you said that you don't want those boys as friends anymore . . ."

"Jacob, I don't—," Rudy started, but Jacob cut him off.

"It is sometimes too hard to get away, even when you want to run. It takes tremendous courage and strength. Not that we don't think you have it. Listen, you know that old Beatles song, 'I get by with a little help from my friends'? We are your friends, and we want you to have an easier life than what you would have without our help."

Rudy was almost in tears and looked to his mama, who was also touched by Jacob's frank display of love toward her son. In this intimate moment, it was as if Jacob truly was his grandpa.

"Julia, Jacob is right. Come on; grant three old men their wishes," Frederick added.

Julia, not knowing how to say no, said, "Alright, yes. But I want to pay you back." Of course, she had no idea how she ever could.

"That is not necessary," Yoshito interjected. "Maya Angelou once said, 'Giving liberates the soul of the giver.' We are the fortunate ones who earn blessings in the giving, as well as you in the accepting. One must let go of their ego to accept a gift, and I applaud your great humility and courage. It is we who thank you."

Julia looked dazed and was beginning to understand why these men had changed her boy so profoundly.

Jacob looked at Rudy again. "It is not easy to start a new school. You will not know anyone; will not have any friends at first. But you will start with a fresh slate. Are you ready to take this step? Are you ready to do the hard work?"

For a split second, Rudy thought about the comfort of the familiar, but then thought about the possibilities that were being laid before him. He considered the changes and risks each of these men had taken in their young lives, the roads they had taken.

"Yes, Jacob. I promised you before that I would try very hard, and I won't disappoint you, or Frederick or Yoshito," and he looked at each of them.

"But school starts in two weeks," Julia interjected.

"I happen to know the principal of the school," Frederick said. "I promised him that Rudy here was a fine young man who would do justice to the school."

"There is much to do though in those two weeks. There are uniforms and books to buy. We will go down Monday and get everything squared away, okay?" Jacob asked.

Julia had tears in her eyes as she hugged and thanked each of them—although "thank you" didn't seem enough. "You are truly God's angels on earth!" she told them.

"Julia, we're just three old men who think your boy is something pretty special," Jacob replied.

As they prepared to go home, Yoshito stepped forward. "Rudy, I have something for you: a thank-you gift for tearing down the fence, an *omiyagi*; something that I want to give you on behalf of all of us."

Rudy came forward, surprise written across his face. Yoshito pulled a leather bag from his pocket that was secured with drawstrings. He reached out for Rudy's hand and put it in his palm.

"What is it?" Rudy inquired.

"Open it and you will see," Jacob teased.

Rudy pinched the bag and pulled it open. He reached in and pulled out an object that was about four inches in diameter and immediately familiar. Flat on one side and rounded glass on the other, Rudy recognized it as a replica of the compass in the garden."

Rudy looked at Yoshito, not quite sure what it meant.

"It was my father's," Yoshito began.

"Yoshito, I can't take this from you."

"My father gave it to me before he died and told me to use it as I navigate through this life. I have kept it with me all these years, and now I no longer need to find my way. I am home and where I want to be. You are just beginning your journey. We have no children or grandchildren to leave it to. I want you to have it on behalf of all of us. I know you will honor it and take good care of it."

Rudy nodded.

Yoshito continued. "This compass is a symbol of many things. It will serve as a reminder to always find your way back home to those who love you, and it will also help you chart your course as you face many moral and ethical dilemmas. Look at it when you need help remembering or knowing what is right and what is wrong."

"It's just like the one on the pedestal," Rudy remarked.

"I told you Yoshito gave me the idea. Remember some ancients thought it akin to the eye of God? I loved its symbolism and had Yoshito's replicated. In its own way, this garden helped us all find our way home," Frederick interjected.

"And maybe, just maybe, it will remind you of your summer with three old men, eh?" Jacob smiled affectionately.

Rudy nodded, not knowing what to say. Everything had happened so fast. His life had changed in a few moments. Following behind his mother, Rudy hugged and thanked Yoshito, reassuring him that he would treasure his *omiyagi*. Then he stepped back and gave Yoshito a slight bow, and said, "*Domo arigatou gozaimasu, Yoshito-san.*"

Yoshito, clearly touched, smiled broadly. "I see my friend was paying attention during his lessons." Rudy could only smile back.

He moved to Frederick, who had been the mastermind behind him getting this summer job. "Frederick, thank you for seeing something in me that even I didn't know I had. Thanks, man." Frederick slapped his back, a gesture that was now familiar and that Rudy had come to expect and love.

Then there was Jacob. Rudy loved them all, but the way he felt about Jacob was the way Dorothy felt about the Scarecrow when she said good-bye and said, "I think I'll miss you most." Rudy suspected this school idea had been his. He hugged Jacob and whispered in his ear, "I love you, Jacob. Thank you."

Flustered and glassy-eyed and unable to reply, Jacob just patted Rudy's cheek affectionately, finally sputtering out, "You're a good boy, Rudy. Now go home and rest up. *Mazel tov.*"

That was all Rudy needed.

As Rudy and his mother walked down the driveway, Rudy reflected that Jacob had been right. For the first time in his life things had all worked out for the best. And Jacob had said it: he was something special. And for the first time, he believed it.

Chapter 17

It was the weekend before school was starting and Rudy, like clockwork, was out working in their paradise early, wanting to savor the last remaining hours with Jacob, Frederick, and Yoshito. Everything was ready for him to start his new school, and he was excited about it, but how he had come to love the long days of summer, with his fingers in the dirt, weeding out the persistent weeds, and planting new growth. He had enjoyed watering the flowers and the vegetables, watching them grow, certain that he heard the whisperings of the plants, just as Yoshito said he would if he opened his mind to it.

This morning Jacob had gone to the nursery on his own while Rudy prepared a patch of ground and dug a big hole for what Jacob had called "something special."

After cultivating the ground, Rudy went over to help Yoshito move some stones into place, and then assisted Frederick with fixing some sprinklers. The men often told Rudy that he could major in landscaping; he had good ideas for design and had come to love the feel of the earth on his skin. Rudy would nod but knew he never wanted to make a job out of this. *This* was fun; this was special and would always be tied to this patch of land and these three men.

Those chores now done, the three of them sat at the bench under the tree drinking their favorite refreshment. Hearing Jacob's car in the front drive, Rudy went out to greet him and saw Jacob struggling to pull something from the back seat.

"Let me help Jacob." Rudy rushed over as the others followed.

"Yes, I think I may need my young Goliath to lift this out. It is too much for an old man like me. Yoshito, the plants at the nursery say hello," he quipped straight-faced.

"What have you got there, Jacob?" Frederick inquired.

Recognizing it, Yoshito said, "Ah, yes, a rosemary plant. It is very big and beautiful. Run your fingers along its leaves and smell, Rudy."

"It smells so good," Rudy said as he breathed in the herbal residue left on his fingers.

Rudy pulled out the large container and carried it to the spot he had cleared.

"It's a pretty plant, Jacob, but what makes it so special?" Rudy asked, remembering the old man's earlier comment.

"The greatest playwright of them all once wrote something about rosemary and what it stands for. Do my educated friends remember?" Jacob asked his longtime neighbors.

"Remember, you're speaking to a literature teacher. In the great words of Mr. William Shakespeare, he said, 'There's rosemary, that's for remembrance; pray, love, remember,'" said Frederick.

"That is correct, my educated friend! This rosemary plant is for remembering. I want to plant it with all of you, as a reminder of this summer—a summer of remembering thanks to our young friend here. I thank you, Rudy, for bringing back my family to me, especially Blanca, who I can now remember without fear, without pain, and without sadness. Now I can remember her laugh and smile and her beauty—thanks to you."

"Yes, it is good to open the wound and let the air circulate around it, otherwise it festers," Yoshito added.

"Gentlemen, I think we would all agree this was a great summer," Frederick chimed in.

"Well, let's get it in the ground!" Rudy said, and then proceeded to pull the plant from its container and check the tightly packed roots for dampness. It was totally dry. Then he lowered the plant into the ground and lovingly filled the hole with water before adding a mixture of soil, peat moss, and mulch. As they watered the top soil, the needled branches glistened in the sun as the spray hit them and held onto each drop.

Yoshito shared that the plant said it liked its new home, thanked Rudy for the water, and was happy to be there. What was more remarkable was that no one thought it was an odd thing to say or doubted that what he said was true.

"We will have to cook something and use the rosemary for seasoning," Frederick said.

Rudy nodded but was thinking about the stories he'd heard and all that had transpired this summer in this place. As he stood in the sun, that hot September Saturday, he knew he would never forget Frederick's father, Yoshito's brother, or Jacob's twin, Blanca. And woven throughout would be his memories of Yoshito creating rivers with raindrops out of pebbles, Jacob's rough and callused hands, Frederick's singing as he worked with his long dead ancestors in the garden, Yoshito's conversations with his plants, Jacob's humor and anguish, his own mother's smile, and fresh pie on a warm summer evening with every person he loved under the great tree. Yes, it was unlikely that he would ever forget one detail of that summer.

Four years later

Chapter 18

It was a weekend at the beginning of spring. Rudy was helping Jacob plant new flowers and refresh the garden after the winter rains had saturated the soil and brought back life from its dormant state. Along with Yoshito, Rudy now claimed he too could hear the plants and flowers rejoicing. Jacob would just smile and tease, "You've been drinking too much of Yoshito's herbal tea. You don't see Frederick or me having conversations with our plants, do you?"

For long hours they would work side by side, sometimes in conversation, sometimes in hours of comfortable silence. Other times they would work as they heard Frederick's rich voice sing out from somewhere in the garden.

"Have you thought anymore about what you want to do with your life? College is just around the corner," Jacob questioned that afternoon.

"You know, I am going to start out at East LA College and try to get the core requirements done before working on any major work. Hopefully I can save enough money with my job at the restaurant and perhaps get some grant money so that I can finish my last two years and any graduate work at a university," Rudy responded as he continued to plant yarrow and rosemary in the beds near the lavender.

"That's a good plan; college takes a lot of money. Have you decided if you want to teach history or literature?" Jacob questioned him further.

"Some days I feel one way, other days I feel the other. I like them both."

"Well, you know how Frederick feels. He wants you to follow in his footsteps. Either way, we'll all be proud. You'll figure it out. There's still time for that," Jacob replied as he stood up and started reaching out for a chair, a lightness in his head and a twinge of pain in his chest.

"I'm tired today. I think I am coming down with something," he continued.

"Go ahead and lay down, Jacob. I can finish up here. After all these years, I think I make a credible gardener." Rudy smiled at the old man. "Here, let me help you," Rudy said as he looked at his old friend, who seemed to be drained of color.

"I'm fine—don't worry about me. You just finish up that bed and then go home and study like a good boy," Jacob smiled and waved even as he was walking toward the back door.

Rudy smiled. Even after all these years, and now that he was eighteen and almost out of high school, Jacob still called him a "good boy." Yes, they had had some mighty good times over the past several years; these men had become grandfathers to him. How he loved them.

Rudy's attention was suddenly diverted toward Jacob's kitchen. He heard a crash. Within seconds, Rudy was up on his feet, rushing into the kitchen only to find Jacob collapsed on the floor. Rudy ran to him, checked his breathing, and tried to rouse him with no luck. He ran to the back door and yelled in the loudest voice he had, "Fred-er-ick! Yo-shi-to! Help me!" Then he ran into the living room to the phone and dialed 9-1-1. He heard the back door slam, and Frederick say, "Oh my God, what happened?" Yoshito following right behind him, took one look and ran to the bedroom and pulled a blanket off Jacob's bed. He came back and covered him while

Frederick went to the bathroom and into the medicine cabinet to look for aspirin.

Rudy was talking to the dispatcher, "Yes, he is breathing, but barely. His color is not so good. He said he wasn't feeling well just minutes before. Yes, yes, we just covered him."

Frederick heard the sirens and went to the front door to meet the paramedics. "I just placed an aspirin under his tongue in case it's his heart," Frederick told one of the attendants.

Rudy hung up the phone to be by Jacob. The men were working on him, so Rudy yelled, "Jacob, do you hear me? Come on, Jacob, come on! I need you. Don't leave me now. I love you!" Rudy cried. Frederick put his arm around him, and Rudy allowed himself to be comforted as if he were a child.

The paramedics hoisted Jacob onto a gurney and wheeled him out to the ambulance with the three others following.

"We're taking him to the hospital. Looks like he had a heart attack. Good thing you gave him that aspirin so quickly."

"I want to go with him," Rudy said.

"Are you related?" the ambulance driver asked?

"Yes, he is family," Yoshito stepped up answering the question before Rudy could. Rudy looked at him with gratitude.

"Okay, get in." Rudy jumped in and sat next to Jacob, and taking his hand, he began talking to him even while the attendant watched various monitors and radioed into the hospital.

"We'll meet you at the hospital," Frederick yelled to him as they closed the back door to the ambulance.

"Not now, not yet, Jacob. Not yet," Rudy pleaded into Jacob's ear.

Chapter 19

Jacob was home but spent most of his time in a chair in the garden watching the others work the soil. He was still too weak to be getting down on the ground. He found that he tired easily, taking many much-needed naps during the day.

Rudy was there as much as possible when he wasn't at school or working at the restaurant. How he wanted to be with Jacob and the others, but he had to earn money for school. But as soon as he could, he always found his way to the garden, even if it was to sit and study with Jacob dozing in the chair next to him. Summer would be here soon, and there would be more time to spend with him.

On this particular day in May, Jacob waited for Frederick and Yoshito to go home. Jacob had a few things he wanted to share with Rudy while he could. He knew his days were coming to an end.

As they talked about school and earning enough money for a university education, Jacob finished the conversation by saying, "Don't worry about it today. Things have a way of working out."

"You always say that," Rudy laughed.

"Yes, but I am always right, aren't I?" Jacob countered, and Rudy acquiesced.

"Rudy, you know it's as if you are my own grandson, and I am so proud of you. You know, I call you a good boy, but I know that you are now a fine young man. No matter what life throws at you, you must stay that way. Promise me, okay?"

"Sure, Jacob. But what's going on?"

"I know I do not have much more time here with you. It's time we had a man to man talk."

"Jacob, don't say that. You survived the heart attack. You're going to be fine; you just need to rest," Rudy pleaded. Jacob put up his hand to silence him.

"Rudy, I could not love you more than I do. Because of you, my life changed for the better in so many ways. For the last four years, I haven't had the nightmares I lived with all my life. I can remember my family without my heart breaking. But I am old and the day will come soon that I will join them, and while I will be sorry to leave you and Frederick and Yoshito and this paradise, I suspect there is an even more beautiful paradise waiting for me with my family. Unfortunately for me, I have to die to get there." Jacob smiled, trying to make light of what he was saying.

"And you, my friend will have some heartbreak to endure. You have come to love three very old men, and the truth is, we will all be gone long before you are just beginning your life, your career, before you have children of your own."

"Don't say that, Jacob." Rudy's eyes were glassy. He didn't want to hear it, but he knew it was true.

"You have been a Goliath. And now you must fight the sadness and bitterness that may come when we are gone. You have heard our stories, Rudy, and you know what we had to overcome. I pray your trials are not as great. But you must move forward and live a full and productive life—and know that three old men thought you were something special."

They sat quietly for a moment then Jacob cleared his throat.

"You know, being a teacher is a fine aspiration. Winston Churchill once said, 'We make a living by what we get, but we make a life by what we give.' As a teacher, you will have a tremendous life, and knowing you, you will give and give and give. That's good."

After a minute, Jacob in an effort to lighten things said, "See, Yoshito is not the only one who can quote things." Together they laughed, and Rudy walked over and embraced Jacob.

"I love you, Jacob.

"I love you, too, Rudy. You're a good boy," and once again Jacob patted his cheek.

Chapter 20

It was a warm October day. Jacob would have liked it. After the funeral, back in the garden, where they had gathered along with his mother, Frederick handed him an envelope.

"Here, Rudy, Jacob left this for you."

Surprised, Rudy walked farther into the garden to the compass where it all began and read the letter alone. It read:

My dearest Rudy,

> *If you are reading this, I have gone home to be with my Father in heaven. I will miss you and the others, but I hope you can be happy for me that after so many decades I am reunited with my family and am free from the shackles that bind us in our earthly life.*
>
> *I want you to remember our talk in the garden many months ago and know that I will be watching as you progress through life. Remember that many wonderful things await you, and that sometimes it comes in the form of a summer job with three old men that you want nothing to do with.*

Frederick and Yoshito and my attorney already know that I am leaving my house to your mother and you. I can't think of anyone else I would rather see in that house and in that garden than the two of you. Your mother has worked hard all her life, and perhaps now with the sale of her house, she will have some money in the bank and not have to worry about a mortgage.

Further, I have left some money to Frederick and Yoshito for the upkeep of the garden. They are old men too, and perhaps they can help another Rudy on his journey.

They are aware that the bulk of my money, I leave to you. You would not think that an old man living in East LA in a rundown neighborhood would have money. But the neighborhood wasn't always that way, and I stayed because of my brothers, for that is what I consider Frederick and Yoshito. I was a successful accountant, invested well, and I think there is enough money to pay for a few years of university education. I want you to have it. The attorneys have it set up in a trust and can help you navigate the legalities. I trust them, and they will do right by you.

I've told you before, but will say it again this final time: I am so proud of you and love you so much. As we part, I will speak the words my father said to me on the last day of his life: "You are a good boy and will be a good man. God is good. Remember that."

Know that I am nearby watching, and one day far in the future, we will meet again in the real Paradise.

All my love, Jacob

As Rudy wept, he folded the letter and laid it against his heart. When he finally tried to put it in his pocket, he felt the now familiar leather bag with the compass that Yoshito had given him. He thought about how he would always find his way back to this place that would now be his home, thanks to Jacob. He also realized that each one of these men had been a compass for him throughout the past four years. Now, one was gone. Rudy wept again, and when he dried his eyes with the calloused hands that were now a badge of honor, he went to find the others. What he saw brought a bittersweet smile to his lips. There, gathered around the rosemary plant, were the people he cared about most. There was his mother, anxiously watching him approach, waiting to comfort him, her red and swollen eyes full of love; then Yoshito, bent over the rosemary plant, listening intently to its whispered conversation; and Frederick, singing out in a joyful voice along with other choral voices that Rudy now heard. In that moment, he heard Jacob's voice telling him not to worry, that things have a way of working out, and he knew it to be true.